JUNE WRIGHT
Faculty of Murder

JUNE WRIGHT (1919–2012) made a splash with her 1948 debut, *Murder in the Telephone Exchange*, whose sales that year in her native Australia outstripped even those of the reigning queen of crime, Agatha Christie. Wright went on to publish five more mysteries over the next two decades while at the same time raising six children. When she died in 2012 at the age of 92, her books had been largely forgotten, but recent championing of her work by Stephen Knight, Lucy Sussex, and Derham Groves, combined with reissues of her novels by Dark Passage Books, has restored Wright to her proper place in the pantheon of crime writers.

LUCY SUSSEX is a novelist and literary historian. Her books include *The Scarlet Rider*, *Matilda Told Such Dreadful Lies: The Essential Lucy Sussex*, *Woman Writers and Detectives in Nineteenth-Century Crime Fiction: the Mothers of the Mystery Genre*, and *Blockbuster! Fergus Hume and The Mystery of a Hansom Cab*. She lives in Melbourne.

Faculty of Murder
MOTHER PAUL INVESTIGATES

JUNE WRIGHT

Introduction by
LUCY SUSSEX

**DARK
PASSAGE**

TO VI

A Dark Passage book
Published by Verse Chorus Press
Portland, Oregon
versechorus.com

Cover design and Dark Passage logo by Mike Reddy
Interior design and layout by Steve Connell Book Design / *steveconnell.net*

Country of manufacture as stated on the last page of this book

Library of Congress Cataloging-in-Publication Data

Names: Wright, June, 1919-2012, author. | Sussex, Lucy, 1957- writer of
    introduction.
Title: Faculty of murder / June Wright ; introduction by Lucy Sussex.
Description: Portland, Oregon : Dark Passage/Verse Chorus Press, [2021] |
    Series: Mother Paul investigates
Identifiers: LCCN 2021043896 (print) | LCCN 2021043897 (ebook) | ISBN
    9781891241413 (trade paperback) | ISBN 9781891241642 (ebook)
Subjects: LCGFT: Novels.
Classification: LCC PR9619.3.W727 F33 2021 (print) | LCC PR9619.3.W727
    (ebook) | DDC 823/.914--dc23
LC record available at https://lccn.loc.gov/2021043896
LC ebook record available at https://lccn.loc.gov/2021043897

Contents

June Wright, with daughter Rosemary, signing copies of *Faculty of Murder*, 1961

INTRODUCTION

The delights of vintage crime-writing have always been known to buffs, but it has taken reprint presses like Dark Passage to reveal them to a larger audience in the twenty-first century. In the process many authors have been rediscovered and reappraised. June Wright is a case in point. She had an international audience for the six novels she published from the late 1940s into the 1960s, with good sales and reviews, but she faded from view when she was obliged to stop writing. While her Australian contemporaries such as A. E. Martin and Charlotte Jay were rediscovered late last century, it was only after Wright's death in 2012 that she was spectacularly rescued from undeserved obscurity.

Wright was an author with a keen sense of place, a regionalist who set her books in Melbourne and Southern Victoria, moreover one who always focused on the feminine. Her preference among the 'Golden Age' canon was always for the women writers. She learnt her craft from reading and applied what she garnered from Mignon G. Eberhart, Dorothy L. Sayers, et al. to her own crime-writing practice.

Faculty of Murder was her penultimate published novel, and the second featuring Mother Paul, her most enduring detective. Nowadays whole websites are devoted to clerical detectives, but in the early 1960s a nun-sleuth was anomalous. Wright had not known of any precursors when she created Mother Paul. She had discarded her first sleuth, Maggie Byrnes, when readers all too readily assumed she was an autobiographical creation; in any case, it would have been difficult to keep on detecting while caring for a growing family, which was the situation in which Wright and Byrnes found themselves in the 1950s. Some of the tensions were evident in Wright's second novel featuring Maggie, *So Bad a Death*, whose working title was, tellingly, 'Who Would Murder a Baby?'

Small wonder then, that Wright created a female detective without children, and married only to a rather less demanding deity. The impetus was an interview with her peer Arthur Upfield, who cited the advantages of an unusual detective. Wright immediately thought of a nun, based on her long and Catholic experience. Mother Paul was a composite figure, and the author's favourite character. She was a 'dear', said Wright.

In this creation, Wright had a winner, and a means of re-booting her publishing career, which had stalled. She had begun well—her debut, *Murder in the Telephone Exchange*, won a Commonwealth competition whose judges included John Creasey—but her pathway was not always assured. She experienced rejections, and had experimented with a psychological thriller, *The Devil's Caress*, before completing *Reservation for Murder,* the first Mother Paul novel.

Around this time she found an ally, a part-time journalist from Bendigo she refers to in her unpublished memoir as 'Mr Davie.' Ray Davie (1921-2012) best known as the Melbourne *Age*'s first and longest-serving real estate editor, was then a radio journalist and aspiring writer. He was also a keen reader, and later reviewer, of crime fiction. Davie had connections with the English publishing and agent world and, more importantly, was about to travel to the UK.

Davie packed the typescript of *Reservation for Murder* in his luggage, arriving in London as Hutchinson & Co., who had published Wright's first three novels but turned down two others, were undergoing a reconstruction. They concentrated their crime portfolio as John Long, and here Wright's three Mother Paul books found their outlet. She also gained a London agent in the process, apparently one of the best in the business.

Wright freely admitted that *Faculty of Murder* was in part inspired by Sayers's *Gaudy Night* (1935), the original academic mystery. Both take place in women's colleges, in Sayers's case a fictionalized version of her Oxford alma mater, Somerville College. Wright had not had the advantage of a university education, then expensive even for the Melbourne middle-class, but she knew Melbourne University, and not only because her eldest children were of an age to be students in the early 1960s. In her memoir she recalls a beau she met through the Newman Society, who took her dancing at the university and drove her through its grounds—a student who was later killed in the war.

She also had a friend who lived at Melbourne University's first Catholic women's college, St Mary's Hall (established in 1918 by the

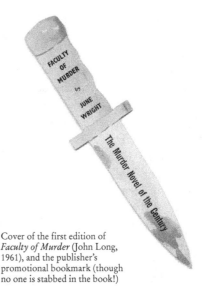

Cover of the first edition of *Faculty of Murder* (John Long, 1961), and the publisher's promotional bookmark (though no one is stabbed in the book!)

Loreto Order), and wrote for radio. Wright's fictional Brigid Moore Hall, founded by an early Catholic feminist, is not St Mary's, but her Manning College is certainly Newman College, simply rechristened after another Cardinal. Both these colleges she merrily situates in the middle of Melbourne General Cemetery, to emphasise their fictional nature. Crucial to the book's plot are the professors' residences scattered through the university grounds, where boundaries between the private and the public, sexual attraction and the pupil-teacher relationship, blur, or are breached.

Though Wright mixed rigorous research with experience for her books, the level of detail in *Faculty of Murder* indicates an informed source, someone who knew the academic gossip. Unlike *Gaudy Night*, Wright's book has a focus on academic philandering. The biggest contemporary Australian scandal of this ilk involved Sydney Sparkes Orr, Professor of Philosophy at the University of Tasmania, who had taught at Melbourne University in the late 1940s and early 1950s. Orr had a penchant for ménages-à-trois involving his students, and while he was sacked for his behaviour in Tasmania, it was not forgotten that he had got a student pregnant at Melbourne. It is likely that the Orr case influenced Wright (though she judiciously limits her fictional Casanova's conquests to staff members).

What would become a link to another Melbourne University sex scandal was the presence of the Gothic tower of Ormond College in the cover design of the original 1961 edition.[1] In the 1990s Ormond hit the news when two female students brought sexual harassment suits against its Master—one consequence of which was *The First Stone* by Helen Garner, a book notorious for castigating the complainants. Compare Wright's approach, fictional, more nuanced, ingenious in its plotting, even wickedly funny: 'The girl was always explaining or interfering in that well-meaning way which regrettably arouses only impotent fury in others. She seemed predestined for welfare work.'

John Long had a local publicist in Melbourne who found Wright a willing subject, despite her express wish that authors should be read rather than seen or heard. A publicity shot shows Wright signing copies of *Faculty*, assisted by her daughter Rosemary. There was also a literary luncheon where each guest got a bloodstained dagger for a bookmark (despite nobody being stabbed in the novel). The book was well-received, with no less than the authoritative Julian Symons terming Mother Paul 'Father Brown's niece.' That amused Wright, who did not greatly care for Chesterton.

As Wright noted in her memoir, if she 'had been able to keep turning out Mother Paul detective novels', she 'would have been set for the rest of her literary life'. Her agent liked the character 'so much', as did her publisher. In the event, she only published one more Mother Paul novel, *Make-up for Murder*, while another remained uncompleted due to family pressures and the need for more paying work. If she regretted her 'stillborn, literary baby,' it was largely because of Mother Paul, and the opportunities the 1960s gave to write about the changing role of nuns following Vatican II. She saw how the character might develop and grow, but would not have the chance to continue with Mother Paul's detecting adventures.

Yet what she did in *Faculty of Murder* arguably shows her writing at its best. June Wright was a superb crime writer, and in this book her

---

1 As Ormond was founded by Presbyterians, that it featured in a book about Catholic colleges was likely not appreciated.

observation, sense of drama, narrative, and above all the inimitable Mother Paul herself are in excellent form.

Lucy Sussex
Melbourne, August 2021

June Wright and daughter Rosemary in the grounds of Melbourne University in 2008, with the tower of Ormond College in the background.

Some alterations have been made to the topography of Melbourne University to suit this fictitious story. May they serve as a guarantee that all characters and incidents too are figments of the author's imagination.

I

Even long after the affair was officially closed it was still discussed. Some incident would be remembered to set off the subject, or there would be someone who had had a slight connexion with it, whose life had been touched by the events at Brigid Moore Hall. It could never be properly talked out, because no one knew precisely what had happened that first term at Melbourne University. No one but the police and a handful of people who only wanted to forget about it.

Sometimes Elizabeth thought it would take years before the clinging aura of murder faded altogether. It still hung about her own life, even though she was not so conscious of it now. Then something would serve to remind her—like that morning towards the end of term when she was having a cup of coffee in the Baillieu Library canteen.

The canteen was full of the clatter and chatter of students and staff enjoying a mid-morning break. Close to Elizabeth's table was a noisy group of undergraduates from Manning College. Suddenly, from behind the effective screen of desert boots, pullovers like half-filled sugar bags and crew-cuts, came Fiona Searle's clear, decisive voice—'No, you boys have got it all wrong! Actually the ghastly business began when Learned Liz came into our rec the first evening looking for the freshettes. Talk about a sensation—Neil, what are you making faces for? Don't you want to hear the inside story? What? Oh . . .'

Elizabeth frowned at the uninviting skin that had formed on her coffee. She spooned the skin aside carefully and lifted the cup. The slight tremor in her hand surprised her. She thought she had got over that long ago.

'Learned Liz'—what an incorrigible brat Fiona was with her sobriquets! It made her sound dull and stuffy. But as a tutor in Humanities with not very many years separating her from the students, there was a need for some sort of surface camouflage. That was why she kept her dark cloudy hair smoothed to a knot in the nape of her neck and wore such clothes as the neat grey suit she had on now.

Suddenly Elizabeth got up and passed by the sheepish faces at the adjoining table with a brief, unsmiling nod. She wanted to get away from the young arrogance of Fiona and her inevitable circle of male students. Let her tell the Manning boys what she liked.

Actually, she mimicked to herself, the ghastly business started over a year ago. But Fiona had always had a good sense of drama, and to begin from that evening in the students' recreation room was as suitable a beginning as any.

Brigid Moore Hall had been founded and endowed by the widow of an illiterate brewer; her practical championship for the cause of tertiary education for Australian women having subsequently been recognized and rewarded by a Papal title. A portrait of the good lady hung in the entrance hall of the college, depicting her in black with a mantilla over her Queen Alexandra coiffure against a dwarfed background of St Peter's Square. The Hall was situated to the north of the University — separated from the actual grounds by a road which cut through east and west between two highways leading out of the city. The back premises, like those of the various professorial and other married staff residences which adjoined the Hall, were lapped by a cemetery.

The Hall consisted of three floors of Victorian Colonial architecture, set in a rambling garden of many trees and shrubs. At one side was a smaller ivy-covered residence which was known as the Cottage. This had been acquired in recent years, its interior having been reshaped to make a fairly large lecture room with an adjoining reading room and laboratory. It also contained two or three small bedrooms, a kitchen, a bathroom and a sitting-room used as a common-room for tutorial staff.

Miss Dove, who frequently referred to this room in such phrases as 'a haven of rest from the rude world', was responsible for the little feminine touches which disguised its conventual austerity. The flowered drapes and cushions, the fluffy lambswool rugs and the clusters of Swan Lake miniatures were all somewhat at variance with her tailored, schoolmistress appearance, and her status as senior tutor in Natural Science.

She and Elizabeth were the only resident tutors, and although disparity in age and outlook made friendship between them impossible, they got on together reasonably well.

Elizabeth had no desire to interfere with her older colleague's home-making efforts. She was engaged to be married and regarded the Cottage only as a temporary dwelling place. But lately she had been wondering gloomily if it would not be a good idea to unpack the various lares and penates stored in the camphor wood chest in her bedroom. Two years was an absurd period of time for a girl to be engaged—not only absurd but humiliating. The next time she saw Timothy she would say so, and make him come to some definite decision about their marriage. Though when she would see him she had no idea. As far as she knew from the two scrappy letters received during the vacation, he was still wandering through the outback of New South Wales looking for stragglers from the Binduk tribe. She would ask him whether he might not prefer to marry a Binduk lubra.

The beginning of a new academic year was always a time of confusion. This year there was not only the hurly-burly of lectures and courses to arrange and the usual crop of freshettes to contend with, but a new Warden had been appointed to Brigid Moore Hall. Old Reverend Mother Raphael had been honourably removed from the post she had fulfilled so zealously for many years and a younger nun had taken her place. Elizabeth saw some harassing weeks ahead while she and the rest of the staff, as Miss Dove put it, helped the new Warden to find her feet.

Summer that year had infiltrated the start of autumn. The sprinklers were turning circles of spray on the lawns and the cicadas were still shrilling raucously in the oak trees as Elizabeth crossed the garden from the Cottage to the main house. It was about seven in the evening and the windows of the students' recreation room in the front part of the house were open to the balmy evening air.

Elizabeth reflected wryly on the subdued and desultory sounds that issued forth, as she skirted the banks of azure-coloured hydrangeas beneath the windows. It would be a different matter in another few weeks when the freshettes too had found their feet, and had ceased to be intimidated by their surroundings and the older students. Even the cicadas would be deafened.

She went into the house, crossed the parquetry hall which the lay sisters kept to a mirror brightness, and paused for a moment on the threshold of the recreation room.

Some of the girls were gathered in groups exchanging holiday stories, but most were standing about aimlessly as though they were uncertain how they came to be there. One student—a tall angular girl in glasses—had withdrawn to a corner with a new-looking textbook up to her large nose and an apple in one hand at which she munched without seeing. She was doing her third year in medicine and was grimly enthusiastic about her career.

Elizabeth came into the room, twitched the book away, then put it back shut into her hands. 'Take it easily, Monica! Exams are a little way off yet. All right, girls! I would like your attention for a few minutes, please.'

Faces turned towards her obediently. They were only too glad to hear the note of authority. One of the older girls, a Social Studies student, who had been trying to organize a table-tennis match at the far end of the room, explained in an audible undertone to the less knowledgeable, 'It's Miss Drew, our Humanities tutor. She wants to arrange about our lectures and things.'

Thank you, Heather,' said Elizabeth dryly.

The girl was always explaining or interfering in that well-meaning way which regrettably arouses only impotent fury in others. She seemed predestined for welfare work.

Elizabeth sat down at a table with a pen and block of paper. 'Now we'll start with students second year and over. I want your full names and Faculties.'

Fiona Searle, who had been picking at a bunch of grapes with a pretty little Asian student, clapped a hand to her mouth. 'Oh, my goodness! What year am I doing now? I did pass, didn't I, Liz?'

'Miss Drew!' said Elizabeth repressively. 'Yes, you managed to scrape through, Fiona. My advice to you this year is to pay more attention to your Arts course, and less to your appearance, social life, and—er—members of the opposite sex.'

Fiona shone a dazzling smile around the room. There was a startling attractiveness about her which came from a background of wealth, clothes, the sighing envy of her fellow students, and the best of imported cosmetics. As she had spent the summer holidays at her parents' beach house on the Peninsula, her peach-smooth skin was richly tanned and her hair fairer than ever. 'That's what you advised last year too,' she agreed cheerfully. 'Oh, well! Back to the grind! I'll be all conscientious and hardworking, a mixture of Heather and Monica.'

Someone—a law student called Nola—said jokingly, 'Oh, don't let us down, Fiona! There's a bet on as to whether you'll become engaged again this year. How many fiancés have you had so far?'

'It's such a shame you don't take your studies as seriously as you should,' declared Heather virtuously. She had a round suety face, spotted here and there with moles like a raisin pudding. 'You know you have got brains, Fiona.'

'Boys are more fun than brains,' returned the other flippantly, tossing a muscatel into the air and catching it in her open mouth.

'That's enough!' ordered Elizabeth, who had been writing busily. 'Who's next?'

Gradually she worked through the list and came to the new students, smiling at them in a friendly fashion. They had separated themselves into an isolated group like a flock of crossbred sheep.

'I've been doing my best to make them feel at home,' muttered Heather Markham. She spoke as though freshettes were an underprivileged unit in society, whose welfare was her cause. They would be grateful to Heather for the first term and then spend the rest of the year trying to avoid her.

'I know you must be feeling rather strange,' Elizabeth said sympathetically. 'It takes a while to become acclimatized to University life. I know that because I was new here once myself. Perhaps you can take comfort in the fact that I became so acclimatized that I'm still here.'

The forlorn faces lightened, and there was a whisper and a giggle among the older students. Elizabeth wondered if they were snickering about her. She could well imagine her long-drawn-out engagement being the butt of rec room wit.

'And now if you will just give me your names and the subjects you are planning to do, so that the Warden can make arrangements about lectures and other matters.' Elizabeth glanced up again. 'Have you met the Warden, by the way? She is new this year like yourselves.'

'Oh, yes, Miss Drew,' the crossbreds chorused, as though relieved to be able to answer something intelligently. One of them added shyly, 'Reverend Mother was in here only a while ago talking to us.'

'Oh, was she?' said Elizabeth, thinking that the Warden could quite easily have done the job she was doing. 'Well, I'm glad you've got to know Mother Paul. I am going to become better acquainted presently. But to get back to your names!'

They gathered around, supplying the information she wanted.

'Well, that seems to be about the lot,' said Elizabeth finally. She put the cap back on her pen and got up. 'Oh, by the way, there is something I missed. Which is our student who won the Florence Ryall?'

Even as she spoke, a flicker of uneasiness darted through her mind. She could not think what had caused the troubled twinge, but her uneasiness grew when a deep little voice replied, 'I won the Ryall scholarship.'

They all turned towards the girl standing apart in the corner of the room. She was small and thin and with bright red hair and a smothering of freckles.

Elizabeth tried to summon up a smile. But there was something about the girl that aroused her apprehensions further—something familiar about the red hair and freckles. 'Well, congratulations! That was a wonderful feat. Let me see now—the last time Brigid Moore had a Ryall scholar was—' Her voice dwindled away as the vague memories and her own words slid together to make an explanation.

Her uneasiness had communicated itself to the rest of the room and the students had advanced silently to stare at the girl with the red hair.

Elizabeth tried to pull herself together. She glanced at the list on her block. 'Oh, yes, you're—what is your name again?'

The girl's slight figure was tensed, and a slow flush crept up under the freckles to clash unbecomingly with her hair. 'Judith Mornane.'

'Mornane!' exclaimed Heather, above the sudden murmurs. 'Why, Miss Drew, wasn't that—?'

'Be quiet!' said Elizabeth curtly. 'Well, congratulations again, Judith. We're proud to have you and I hope you'll be very happy here.' She consulted her notes again. 'You're planning to do Science, aren't you?'

The girl seemed to swallow nervously. 'Yes, I'm going to do Science,' she replied, hardly above a whisper. 'And I'm going—going to find out—'

'Find out what?' asked Elizabeth sharply.

The freshette held her head high. She looked round the circle of watching faces.

'Speak up, ducky!' requested Fiona nonchalantly. 'We're all agog.'

Gripping her hands together as though to brace herself, Judith Mornane said clearly and deliberately, 'I'm going to find out who murdered my sister Maureen.'

2

'Did the announcement cause a sensation?' asked the Warden. 'What did the students say?'

'No one said a word,' replied Elizabeth breathlessly. She had finally found Mother Paul in the Cottage library, drifting up and down the shelves with the contented air of an inveterate browser. Her serenity remained unimpaired and she continued to run one hand along the contents of the shelves even after the disturbing story Elizabeth told her.

Presently she paused in her perambulations, pulled out a book, turned its leaves, then replaced it lovingly. 'No comments—either of concern or ridicule? How odd!'

Elizabeth tried to keep a tart note out of her voice. 'We were all too dumbfounded to speak. It is my belief the Mornane girl merely wanted to attract attention. Occasionally we get freshettes like that. Fiona Searle used to make the most ridiculous assertions until everyone became accustomed to her.'

Mother Paul pulled out another book. 'What a delightful library this is! I wonder who is responsible for its admirable order?'

'I am,' replied Elizabeth shortly, irritated by the new Warden's irrelevancy. Mother Raphael, the previous Warden, would have given her closest and gravest attention.

Mother Paul replaced the second book with a sigh. 'But do you think that the girls will ever become accustomed to the assertion that one of them is a murderess?'

'No, of course not,' replied Elizabeth, with the vague feeling of having been caught out somewhere, 'which is why I came to tell you about the girl at once. If she were to receive a severe reprimand from the right quarter she would soon take back this appalling accusation. She could say she was only joking or something like that.' Elizabeth felt a strange compulsion to add this rider. The girl had seemed so scared; there had been something pathetic about her determination to speak.

The Warden moved over to the window and flipped the Venetian blinds open and shut as though the testing of their efficiency were part of her new post. 'I sometimes find that a severe reprimand is just the thing needed to harden one in one's original resolution,' she said softly.

'That is true,' agreed Elizabeth reluctantly. 'What do you suggest should be done then?'

A sudden sweet and disarming smile banished the absent expression from Mother Paul's face. Elizabeth felt the warmth of an unusual personality hidden behind the impersonal garb and demeanour of a religious. She could not help smiling back.

'Yes, so much better to be friends,' said the Warden, with engaging candour. 'And so difficult to step into the shoes of such a wonderful and saintly person as dear Mother Raphael. Comparisons are inevitable.'

'I hope I haven't given the impression that I resent your having taken her place,' said Elizabeth, in some confusion.

'Of course not, dear child. May I call you Elizabeth? Such a beautiful name—the Baptist's Mother or the Queen of Hungary? But I must not digress and waste precious time. We can't have murders being committed at the University—students are here to study, not to be killed.'

'But there wasn't a murder,' protested Elizabeth, shocked. 'Well, no body, anyway. Maureen Mornane simply disappeared. The police went thoroughly into the case and their conclusion was that she did so for reasons best known to herself. Young Judith's inference that someone here disposed of her sister's body after murdering her is simply ludicrous.'

'Supposing you tell me what happened this time last year,' suggested the nun. 'What sort of girl was Maureen Mornane?'

Elizabeth hesitated. 'Well, I only saw her once or twice in the three days she was at Brigid Moore. She had red hair and freckles like Judith, but she seemed a quiet unobtrusive girl. I do recall one thing dearly though—she walked with a slight limp.'

'What course was she planning to do?' asked the nun, poking at the bowl of early dahlias Miss Dove had arranged on the window ledge.

'Science—the same as Judith. They must come from a clever family. They both won the Florence Ryall residency. I only hope there are no more Mornane girls—the two we've known have been more than enough.'

'Where do they come from? Are there parents?'

'They live in the Wimmera district somewhere. Maureen's father came down when the inquiries about her disappearance started.' Elizabeth smiled faintly as she added, 'I remember his saying what a bad time Maureen chose—that she should know they were in the middle of harvesting.'

'How odd! Wasn't his daughter's whereabouts more to him than wheat?'

Elizabeth propped herself against the old-fashioned marble fireplace so as to command a continuous view of the Warden's movements. 'He thought Maureen was just up to some trick. It transpired she was a bit of an imp at home.'

'And without any doubt the police took his attitude into account,' nodded the nun. 'But what about you, Elizabeth? Did you consider the child would have run away just for a trick?'

The girl drew her brows together. 'I tell you I didn't know her properly at that early stage. All freshettes seem alike at the beginning of the year.'

Mother Paul turned in a billow and rustle of voluminous black serge skirts. 'You mean but for the red hair, the limp and the Ryall scholarship, you would not remember Maureen? What about the students? Would they know more about her?'

'They might, but you know what girls of that age are like. When Maureen disappeared they all said something different. One version was that she seemed to have some dreadful sorrow on her mind—another was that she was frightened about something.'

'And the police discounted them?'

'Naturally they did.'

The nun sighed again. 'A great pity that people will tend to embellish the facts. Exaggerations frequently contain some germs of truth.'

'Young Judith's assertion that her sister was murdered is an exaggeration,' declared Elizabeth roundly. 'But there is certainly no germ of truth.'

'I hope you may be right. Such an odd situation! But much less harmful to examine the facts dispassionately than to dismiss the poor child's notion out of hand. Don't you agree, my dear?'

'Yes—yes, I suppose so.'

The nun beamed happily at the endorsement, reluctant though it was. 'Good! Now let me see if I have the facts correctly. Maureen Mornane won the Florence Ryall scholarship, travelled from her country home in the Wimmera to Melbourne where she entered Brigid Moore Hall to study Science. She seemed a quiet unobtrusive girl to her seniors, but of a somewhat secretive disposition to her fellow students. I daresay secretiveness is what the students really meant. Such an odd lopsided picture when you consider that Maureen's father gave the impression she was high-spirited and mischievous.'

'But to continue—after three days in residence at Brigid Moore, where she apparently led a normal freshette's existence, Maureen disappeared without trace or reason.' The Warden looked across at Elizabeth, whose brows had again twitched together in a frown.

'What is troubling you, dear? Something I have stated incorrectly—or perhaps left unsaid?'

Elizabeth stood upright and went back to the table. 'No—no, nothing like that. There was something I omitted. A small matter perhaps, but I only learned of it some time after the police inquiries had died down. Everyone agreed that Maureen disappeared on the fourth day after breakfast—she wasn't at her lectures that morning. But she was still within the environs of the University. Miss Dove told me she was sure she caught a glimpse of Maureen about mid-morning. She did not say anything to the police because at the time she was not certain.'

'Where did Miss Dove catch this glimpse?'

But before Elizabeth had time to reply the door was pushed open wider and a voice interrupted brightly, 'Listeners never hear any good of themselves, so I'd better make my presence felt.' Miss Dove, her academic gown slung loosely over the shoulders of her beige linen dress, came in.

'Ah, good evening. Reverend Mother! That little busybody, Heather Markham, told me about the furore in the youngsters' rec. What is going to be done about the matter? Mother Raphael would have given the girl short shrift, I assure you.'

Elizabeth glanced apologetically at the new Warden, who only asked mildly, 'Is that what you consider I should do?'

Miss Dove gave her gown a hitch. 'Definitely! A stitch in time saves nine, I always say. The child must be mad to make such an outrageous accusation. I feel sure. Reverend Mother, that if you were to threaten her with expulsion we'd hear no more nonsense.'

'You think that Judith Mornane's suggestion that her sister met with foul play is nonsense?'

Miss Dove stared. 'Of course! And as to her further suggestion that someone here murdered her sister—why, the idea belongs to the realm of fantasy or detective fiction. Maureen Mornane disappeared for her own very good reasons.'

Though Elizabeth had subscribed to the same theory just as vehemently only a short time previously, she now found herself saying, 'You know, the more I think of it, the less reason I can find for Maureen's having a good reason.'

Avoiding her colleague's incredulous stare and the faint twinkle in the Warden's eyes, she added, 'She was obviously a keen student—winning the Florence Ryall is a splendid effort.'

Miss Dove gave a delicate snort. 'Was she so frightfully keen? Certainly I only had her for one class, but she didn't impress me as being brilliant.'

The Warden, who had been listening intently, asked with deceptive meekness, 'If Miss Drew can suggest a reason why Maureen should not have disappeared voluntarily, perhaps you can put one forward why she should, Miss Dove.'

Elizabeth silently and reluctantly applauded the nun's shrewdness, which, however, was doing nothing to solve the inner conflict she was experiencing. There was a sudden frightening uncertainty about everything, which somehow stemmed from the serene figure of the Warden herself.

A slight flush had appeared under Miss Dove's smooth, sallow skin. She turned away to rearrange the dahlias on the window sill. 'Yes, Reverend Mother, I can put forward a suggestion. I saw Maureen Mornane coming out of the Craskes' front gate next door the day Mrs Craske was found accidentally drowned in her bath.'

The nun's angelic blue eyes widened and her brows shot up to her coif.

'Helena Craske had been an invalid for years,' explained the senior tutor, standing back to inspect the effect of her flower arrangement. 'Either she fainted while taking a bath or the drugs she had been in the habit of using caused unconsciousness. I believe the post-mortem revealed she was full of phenobarb.'

'Poor soul—what a shocking business!' remarked the Warden, with the vagueness that Elizabeth had come to suspect.

'Well, they say accidents will happen even in the best-regulated circles,' pronounced Miss Dove briskly. 'But you are wondering about Maureen Mornane, Reverend Mother. My suggestion is simply that Maureen found Mrs Craske dead and got such a hearty fright that she panicked into running away. Helena's body was not discovered until nearly lunchtime at which hour young Maureen was well and truly off the scene.'

She faced the Warden and Elizabeth to inspect the effect of her words this time.

The nun nodded slowly. 'That would be possible, don't you agree, Elizabeth? What did the police say to your theory, Miss Dove?'

A defensive expression touched the tutor's face and she moved across to the mantelpiece to check her watch with the glass-covered pendulum clock. 'I didn't tell the police my theory,' she replied, over her shoulder. 'Neither Mrs Craske's death nor Maureen's disappearance was any of my business. Professor Craske had enough to worry about, without my adding to his troubles. Least said, soonest mended is my motto.'

Nobody spoke for a moment.

'Perhaps I was mistaken in seeing Maureen coming out of the gate,' went on Miss Dove, as she moved the mantelpiece ornaments about haphazardly. 'Perhaps she was only passing and touched it the way some people keep touching fences as they walk along a footpath. It was only by chance that I glanced out of the lab window which overlooks the Craske garden. I could see across the shrubs and things to the gate.'

'Did Maureen know Professor or Mrs Craske?'

'She knew Professor Craske, I suppose,' replied Miss Dove

off-handedly. 'As she was doing Science she must have attended a couple of his lectures even in the short time she was here. I don't know about Mrs Craske—did any of the girls go to Helena's under-grad teas, Miss Drew?'

'Some of them went, but I don't know about Maureen. It seems unlikely, as she was a freshette.'

'Could Maureen have called in to consult Professor Craske on some matter relating to her course?' suggested the Warden.

'No, she couldn't have done that,' replied Miss Dove roundly. 'Where she should have been at that hour was in the Prout Lecture theatre listening to him.'

'Professor Craske was lecturing at the University at the time when his unfortunate wife fainted in the bath?'

'Yes, he left home about eight-thirty that morning and did not hear about Helena until lunchtime. The daily help found her and came yelping in here for assistance. At that time Professor Craske was in conference with one of the Deans in the Science department. I know, because I broke the news to him there myself.'

'A distressing task to have to perform,' remarked the Warden, an innocuous little phrase which aroused only foreboding in Elizabeth.

She shot a quick troubled glance at her senior colleague. Didn't she realize that her recital of the facts sounded too obvious an attempt to establish an alibi for Richard Craske? It was not only foolish but unnecessary. There had been no hint of—of— Why, at the inquest, the coroner had expressed his sympathy to the bereaved husband.

Elizabeth quelled a small tremor of her pulse. The rash statement blurted out by an insignificant little freshette now seemed like a pebble dropped into murky stagnant waters.

'But why,' she heard herself asking, almost without volition, 'hasn't Maureen Mornane returned? She can't still be in a panic after twelve months—that is, presuming she did happen to find Helena Craske dead.'

The Warden nodded approvingly, but Miss Dove swung round and said with something of a snap, 'I think all this discussion is getting us nowhere. The police were informed about Maureen—it is their job to find her whether she is hiding of her own accord or not. Reverend Mother's job is to nip young Judith's nonsensical notions in the bud.'

Elizabeth looked uncomfortably at the nun.

The absent expression descended on Mother Paul's face again. She put her head on one side, listening to the bell being tolled by a member of her community from the main house.

'*A la bonne heure!*' she murmured, to the mystification of her Natural Science tutor who thought she was uttering some routine aspiration. 'I must go now. I will endeavour to deal with the situation as it seems best for all concerned, Miss Dove. In the meantime—' she caught Elizabeth's eye with an almost imperceptible twinkle— 'Sufficient unto the day is the evil thereof.'

Elizabeth decided that much as she deplored the new Warden's ideas, she was going to find her delightful company.

3

The dumbfounded silence which followed Judith Mornane's desperately spoken announcement in the students' recreation room lasted only until Elizabeth's departure.

It was Fiona who broke the tension. There was a hint of malice in the mischievous sparkle of her blue eyes. 'But how fantabulous!' she exclaimed gleefully. 'Maureen's kid sister come to play the avenging angel! Which one of us do you suspect?'

The other freshettes had moved away from Judith, unhappy and puzzled by the shattering climax to an already strange day. She was left standing awkwardly alone to face the ridicule that was inevitable now that Fiona had sounded the note of derision.

'But of course Maureen was murdered! Why ever didn't I think of it before? Merely disappearing is frightfully feeble. You must let me help you. I'd simply adore looking for clues.'

The younger girl's face was scarlet. She was close to tears already. 'You might have—have done it,' she jerked out fiercely.

Fiona's eyes widened. 'But of course I might have. That's why I've offered my valuable assistance—so as to put you off the right trail. You can't possibly suspect your fellow sleuth—it simply isn't done.'

Judith dashed a hand across her eyes. 'Maureen was my sister. Don't you dare make a joke about her.'

'My dear. I'm not joking. Only think—a killer in our midst.' She gave a dramatic shiver. 'We must find out who she is before she has time to strike again.'

'I'll put my money on you as the next victim, Fiona,' offered one of the girls.

'Ah, yes,' agreed Fiona mysteriously. 'That's because I know more than is good for my safety. Unbeknownst even to me I hold that small but fatal clue—the key to the whole mystery. What can I do to wrench it from my subconscious mind? Come on, you psychology students, help your poor haunted and hunted pal.'

'You really know something?' stammered Judith eagerly. 'Please, you must tell me!'

Fiona strode up and down the room, with clenched hands pressed to her temples. 'What is it I know? How I wish I could remember! It must come to me—it must!'

'Lay off, can't you, Fiona? The child thinks you mean it,' said the medical student in her sparse abrupt voice. 'I vote we forget what Judith said. What do you say, girls? She must know she was only talking rot, anyway.'

'I know what prompted that suggestion, Monica,' said Fiona accusingly. 'You don't deceive me for a moment. If I were Judith I would regard your apparently friendly intervention with the gravest suspicion.'

The other girl only grinned and threw her book across the room. 'You little wretch, Fiona,' she said, without rancour.

Fiona returned the book neatly. 'Wasn't it last year you told us all those grisly stories about the dissecting room?'

'By golly, yes!' cut in the law student named Nola. 'And you were complaining about the lack of corpses, Monica—only one body to about a dozen students. How's that for a good and subtle motive, Fiona?'

'Terrific! We must check and see if the Anatomy school hasn't a red-haired female hidden away on ice somewhere.'

'Don't be a dope!' said Monica scornfully. 'If I wanted a corpse to experiment on, I'd do a Burke and Hare over our back wall—not commit murder.'

Fiona strolled back to their unfortunate butt. 'Don't you take any notice of Monica, Judith,' she advised kindly. 'She's still trying to put you off the scent.'

'I think you're all horrible—just horrible!' the girl cried, unable to hold back the tears any longer. She rushed out of the room, banging the door behind her.

There was an uncertain silence. Then Fiona gave a little embarrassed shrug. 'She shouldn't have said what she did. Who does she think she is, anyway?'

Monica went back to her corner chair and opened her book. 'Poor kid! She'll learn.'

One of the freshettes forced a laugh. 'I hope you won't think the rest of us are as crazy.'

Fiona gave the speaker a candid scrutiny. 'We're not likely to think of you at all,' she assured her.

'Oh, Fiona! How rude!' said Heather Markham sadly, belatedly coming to the rescue of one freshette. 'Not everyone is as ready to take a joke as you are.'

'Was I joking?' asked Fiona indifferently. 'Nola, what about a game of ping-pong? I just feel like bashing something.'

'Same here! What a start to term!'

They moved away to the end of the room, leaving Heather with her prim mouth buttoned up disapprovingly. 'I think I'd better go after that poor girl and find out what the trouble is. I didn't like to interfere before as she seemed so wrought up. The police didn't seem to think anything really terrible could have happened to Maureen.'

Monica lifted her head. 'You're a fool if you do. If she knows she's got a sympathizer, there'll be no end to her imaginings.'

Heather shook her head gravely. 'I can't bear to think of anyone in trouble without trying to help. It's funny of me, I know, but I just happen to be made that way.'

'It is for the Warden to do something,' declared Monica, in her forthright manner. 'I bet Miss Drew hasn't lost much time telling her about the cuckoo in our nest. The poor kid might get booted out if she's not careful.'

'That's precisely what I intend to point out to Judith,' nodded Heather. 'If she'll only confess to me that she was speaking wildly. I'm sure I'll be able to intervene on her behalf with the Warden.'

'Bless your officious little heart!' Fiona called after her. 'For myself, I'd prefer a ton of teasing.'

'Ah, yes—but you're different, Fiona,' replied Heather, then bustled out of the room in search of her latest welfare victim.

No one relied upon Heather having any success. But confidence was placed in the new Warden's being able to do something to dispel the atmosphere of uneasiness and insecurity that had settled on Brigid Moore Hall. Mother Paul's appearance in the students' dining-room next morning was anxiously awaited.

She came gliding in as breakfast was being served by the two rosy-cheeked lay sisters who constituted the domestic staff.

'I know comparisons are odious,' muttered Miss Dove to Elizabeth at the table they shared at one end of the room, 'but I can't help wishing there was a stronger hand at the helm just now. Mother Paul seems too vague and unsure, if you know what I mean.'

'Perhaps,' replied Elizabeth wickedly, 'we are making a mountain out of a molehill.'

She glanced across at the students' table.

Judith Mornane was sitting at one end, looking subdued and suspiciously swollen about the eyes. No one seemed to speak to her, and she was only picking at the fried sausages and bacon the others were consuming with gusto. Then Fiona threw a remark down the line of girls of which Elizabeth caught the word 'poison'. The laugh that followed and the glares at Judith told her that the girl was being taunted mercilessly.

The Warden made her way slowly round the room, beaming fondly on her charges, as she spoke a few words here and there. She showed no sign of anxiety or haste, and seemed oblivious to the air of expectancy in the room when she came to Judith.

The girl made to rise, but the Warden pressed her down again and pushed forward a rack of toast. 'That's right—eat a good meal. So important when you are studying.' She pressed the girl's shoulder again and then went on to the next student.

'Procrastination is the thief of time,' muttered Miss Dove disgustedly, as Mother Paul presently left the room without a word on the matter that was uppermost in everyone's mind.

Not only did the Warden give the appearance of having forgotten the disturbance of the previous evening, but she showed not the slightest surprise or disapproval when Judith Mornane sought her out after breakfast.

There was a small box-like room opening from the hall of the main house which was used as an office. There the new Warden sat, turning over neat piles of papers which her predecessor had left as a guide to the conduct of Brigid Moore Hall affairs.

Mother Raphael must have spent the eve of her departure feverishly jotting down hundreds of helpful hints which were an accumulation of her experience as Warden. Being given to cryptic utterances herself. Mother Paul had no difficulty in following such items as 'four eggs a week' — 'Burke on Torts'. She knew Mother Raphael meant that the girls' health depended on a certain intake of protein and that Burke's textbook was evidently the best for the law students.

She glanced up over her horn-rimmed glasses as Judith Mornane appeared hesitantly on the threshold of the office, and bade her come in and shut the door so as to cut off the noise of the polishing machine Sister Lydia was wielding over the parquetry.

'Everything comes to him who waits . . . Dear me, such a catching habit! The irritating ones always are. But shouldn't you be at a lecture, Judith?'

The girl gulped nervously. She seemed on the verge of another momentous declaration. 'I didn't want to go — I couldn't! Reverend Mother, I want to leave Brigid Moore.'

The Warden took off her glasses, slid them into a mysterious slit of her voluminous robes, then surveyed her visitor thoughtfully. Presently she said in a coaxing tone, 'Come, child — why not tell me the whole story? I must confess I was hoping you would come to me. As I'm sure the good Miss Dove would also say — two heads are better than one.'

Judith sniffed wetly and stared through tear-filled eyes. Two heads — ? You mean you don't want me to leave? You think something did happen to my sister — that she couldn't have disappeared and left no trace of her own accord?'

'Well, you seem to believe so — in fact, from what I've been told, you were quite forthright on the matter,' returned the Warden.

Judith hung her bright head. 'I was a fool. I don't know what possessed me to blurt out what I did. No wonder everyone is so angry with me, but — '

'Yes, you were foolish,' interrupted the nun cheerfully. 'Far better if you had come to me first to discuss the matter quietly.'

The girl looked at her abjectly. 'Yes, I realize that now. But I didn't expect — what I mean is, the police — '

'You didn't expect me to have an open mind on such a terrible possibility as murder — especially as the police are apparently convinced your sister's whereabouts are her own affair?'

Judith nodded and smiled wanly. 'I felt it was me against — against the world. Making a scene was the only way to—to help Maureen. My family are quite resigned now, you know.'

'Are they? Well, wipe your eyes, my poor child, and tell me why you alone are so convinced that something terrible has happened to your sister. That was a very grave accusation you made.'

The girl brought out an already sodden handkerchief obediently. 'I can't tell you exactly—but I just feel it.' Maureen wouldn't have disappeared of her own free will.'

The Warden sighed and compressed her lips. 'Yes, I know what you mean, dear. But all the repetition in the world won't make facts out of feelings. If we are to do anything either to justify your terrible conviction or to remove your uncertainty, we must work from facts. So mundane, but so necessary, I find.'

The girl looked abashed. 'I'm sorry, but—well, I just have to say it—I feel that something or someone here at Brigid Moore must have changed Maureen.'

'So contradictory of me,' said the Warden apologetically, 'but that is one feeling I am interested in. Perhaps if you were to listen to what I have been told of your sister, it might help clarify your ideas. First of all, she was not unlike you in appearance.'

'She wasn't a bit like me,' declared Judith. 'Neither of us thought so. Why, she was shorter for one thing.'

'Close relatives always find difficulty in seeing resemblances—but, child, your hair and your—er—skin!'

'You mean my freckles? Oh yes, I'm sorry. Perhaps we were alike there.'

'Both Miss Drew and Miss Dove found Maureen quiet and un-obtrusive, the latter being a little disappointed with her intellectual ability. More is evidently expected of a Ryall scholar—Nota bene, child! The girls found her a bit more than unobtrusive—from what I can gather she struck them as being somewhat secretive. Oh—and one other point, I believe Maureen walked with a limp.'

Judith nodded. 'She was kicked by a horse years ago and some bone or other didn't knit properly. But, Reverend Mother, Maureen wasn't shy and secretive. She was always friendly and gay and full of spirits. She was so looking forward to the University. That's why I feel someone here must have changed her. Do you think she was frightened of something? Yet she wasn't afraid of anything as a rule — she would do anything for a dare. Oh, I can't understand!'

The nun rose with a rattle of wooden beads and paced up and down the small room. 'Sit down, my dear. I always think better when I move about.'

Judith took her vacated chair and pulled the folds of her undergraduate's gown over her knees. Her eyes, fixed on the Warden, were hurt and puzzled but hopeful.

'Tell me, Judith, did Maureen ever mention any of her fellow-students in her letters? Or members of the University staff? She was doing Science, wasn't she? Did she ever write anything about Professor Craske, for instance?'

The girl shook her head slowly. 'We only had the one letter from her. She started it on the train coming down and posted it from here as soon as she arrived. She wouldn't have had time to get to know anyone.'

The nun wheeled round, the edge of her veil brushing some of the previous Warden's papers from the desk. 'But you said she was a friendly girl.'

Judith bent to pick up the papers. 'Yes — yes, I know. Truly she was! I tell you something happened here to change her — something terrible.' She paused, her thin, childish hands nervously assembling the papers into alignment like a pack of playing cards. 'Why did she forget to carve the sign? I looked everywhere but I couldn't find it. That girl Heather said I have the room Maureen used. Only some terrible trouble could have made her forget. She remembered it at boarding-school and she was in scrapes there from the first day. On the very morning she left home she said to me, "Do you know the first thing I'm going to do when I hit Brigid Moore, Ju? Lay the mark of the Mornanes so that next year you'll find it."'

'Hush, dear child!' said the Warden soothingly, as Judith finished on a tearful gulp. 'Here, take my handkerchief and explain to me about this — er — mark of the Mornanes.'

Judith accepted the handkerchief gratefully and blew her small, freckled nose. 'It was a game Maureen and I started as children. I think we got the idea from Hansel and Gretel — you know, how Hansel dropped pebbles to show the way home. There is a lot of wild, timbered country where we live and you can easily get lost—especially children playing. Maureen used to carve a mark—a circle with a diagonal cross inside—on the trees. She would have a start and my part of the game would be to find the marks and catch up with her.'

'And so you've been finding her sign and catching up ever since,' said the Warden gently. 'I see. What fun you had together!'

'I made up my mind that if I couldn't find the mark of the Mornanes, I would speak up about Maureen. I know it sounds silly but—well, I thought there might be a chance of someone betraying herself.'

'Miss Drew told me they were dumbfounded,' said Mother Paul, but she added softly, 'Perhaps no one spoke because, in their hearts, they too are not quite happy as to what happened to Maureen.'

Judith stared at her with wide, awed eyes. 'You mean there's a chance one of them might have—could have—' her frightened whisper died away.

'No chance, I hope,' replied the Warden matter-of-factly, wanting to subdue the girl's alarm. There was nothing to be gained from arousing her hopes and fears unduly. 'We have a long way to go yet. First of all we must find out what caused the change in your sister's behaviour. Have you still got that letter she wrote?'

Judith shook her head. 'Daddy gave it to the police and they did not return it.'

Mother Paul considered this piece of information a good sign that the police were far from considering Maureen Mornane's case closed. But she merely answered vaguely, 'How odd! I'll ask about it when I go and see the officer who handled the case.'

Judith blinked. Then a weak twinkle broke up the anxiety on her young face. 'Oh, Reverend Mother, do you really intend visiting the police?'

The nun looked surprised, 'Why not, dear child? It seems a reasonable move—to consult the police first.'

The girl stifled a giggle. 'Won't it be considered a bit—odd?'

'I don't see why. But there is one matter causing me some concern. I don't think Mother Tobias would care to accompany me on such an excursion. I wouldn't dream of upsetting her further—so difficult to get used to a new superior at the best of times.'

'I'll come with you,' offered Judith.

'No, not you, dear. I think I'll ask Miss Drew. She seems not only clever, but discreet. I wonder why she doesn't smile as much as she should? Engaged too! So much wiser for you to stay out of things, Judith—at least until your little foolishness is forgotten.'

Judith's face brightened further. 'Do you think it will be forgotten? I can see now that I couldn't have done a stupider thing. But please, Mother Paul, I would like to help.'

'So you shall—but not just yet. What I want you to do for the moment is to behave as a normal student. Aren't the girls' practising for the Commencement sports over at the Oval? Go and join them.'

'They wouldn't want me—except to jibe at.'

'Yes, they would. The teasing will soon stop if you go quietly about your ordinary life. So please, child, no more startling announcements.'

A preoccupied expression settled on Mother Paul's face after Judith had gone. Presently she began exploring the drawers of her desk until she found what she wanted—a notebook. She was a great believer in committing facts to paper.

4

IT was inevitable in an enclosed community such as a University that rumours should spread concerning the fracas at one of its colleges. However, being Commencement time, when a traditional spirit of levity was rife in undergraduate circles, the rumours were regarded as stemming from a student prank.

Elizabeth had spent part of the morning at Manning, one of the men's colleges. Owing to the general shortage of staff, there was an arrangement between Manning and Brigid Moore for an interchange of tutors. She circled the University Oval on her way back to the Hall for lunch, idly watching groups of students of both sexes in vivid track suits practising for the Commencement sports.

'Hullo, Miss Drew!' panted Fiona, pacing inside the fence on incredibly long, slim legs topped by minute running shorts. 'See who's over there throwing a javelin? What a terrific murder weapon it would make!'

'That's silly talk,' replied Elizabeth coldly.

But Fiona merely grinned and waved an unchastened hand. 'Bye, now! Don't eat all the Colombo Plan hash. I'll be starved after this work-out.' She dashed away stylishly.

Elizabeth strolled on, shading her eyes. She caught sight of a flaming head in the middle of the ground, and presently leaned on the railing to watch Judith Mornane being coached in the art of javelin throwing by an instructor from the Beaurepaire Centre.

'Good afternoon, Miss Drew!'

Elizabeth half-turned. 'Why, hullo Margaret! I missed seeing you this morning. How have you been?'

A trim little woman with a round, youngish face under a cap of prematurely white hair put down a heavy shopping basket. She was the housekeeper at Manning College.

'Oh, just so-so, you know. Terribly busy, of course. You think you'll never get organized at the beginning of the year.'

Elizabeth smiled pleasantly. 'Yes, I get that feeling too.'

Miss Knight smoothed the gloves over her small, capable hands. A derogatory note sharpened her voice. 'Oh, it's very different being on the teaching staff. It's us poor domestic slaves that really have the hard work. Only think—I spent all yesterday morning moving beds! Just as well I'm a strong person.'

'Couldn't you find anyone to help?' asked Elizabeth, with idle amiability.

Miss Knight tossed her neat milky head scornfully. 'By the time I found anyone capable enough, I could finish the job. But what can you get nowadays in the way of domestics? They're all after higher education, if you please.'

'Oh well, it's very laudable!' murmured Elizabeth.

'Higher education!' pronounced Miss Knight with disdain. 'I'm sick of the word, believe you me. Look at all these girls now. They don't know how lucky they are—born with silver spoons, every one of them. They don't have to work for their livings from fourteen. All they think of is books and games and boys to admire them.'

She bent down and picked up her basket. 'Oh well, I've had my little moan! Now I'd better get going and see what sort of mess those maids of mine are making of lunch. Cheerio, Miss Drew!'

'Good-bye,' returned Elizabeth, preparing to move on too.

But Miss Knight turned back, as though she had thought of something suddenly. 'By the way, what's this I hear about your college? I never did think it healthy—a lot of women living together with their noses in books or squinting at bits of frogs' insides. It's not natural, I always say. Someone's bound to act silly.'

Odd, how women like Margaret are always hard on their own sex and over-tolerant with the opposite sex, thought Elizabeth. She replied coldly, 'Yes, one of the girls has been a little foolish. The Warden is dealing with her.'

'What's she like—the new Warden? I heard she's a dithery old duck.'

'Reverend Mother is a charming, scholarly woman.'

Miss Knight shifted the basket to her other arm. 'My, my! Have I said the wrong thing? I'm sorry. I'm sure. But I didn't dawdle to chat about her ladyship. Those bad lads of mine,' her sharp voice took on an indulgent note when she spoke of the Manning students, 'are planning a rag—a skit on the Missing Mornane they call it. That's that girl who did a bunk last year. I shouldn't be telling you, really—I promised I wouldn't, but I thought you might like to be prepared.'

'I think you should be informing the Rector, not me,' suggested Elizabeth, annoyed.

'Oh, go on! I'm not such a spoil-sport. They're only young once. Well, I must be off. Bye-bye, again!'

With compressed lips, Elizabeth watched the housekeeper's sprightly figure disappear. Then she turned and walked swiftly back to Brigid Moore.

Skirting the main house by a path through the shrubbery, she heard her name called for the third time. 'I haven't seen you since the holidays, Elizabeth. Do stop and pass the time of day with an old and valued friend.'

She recognized the smooth, subtly caressing voice at once and looked about for its owner.

'Over here—among these blasted thorny roses! Let's natter over the fence like a couple of suburban housewives.'

'I'm afraid I haven't got time to stay. Professor,' answered Elizabeth, recognizing a figure among the foliage. Any other man would have looked a little foolish in that setting, but Richard Craske always managed to preserve his air of insouciance under any conditions. His nonchalance and well-preserved Greek-god appearance, more than his excellent academic qualifications, made his lectures well-attended by budding female scientists.

'Professor!' he mimicked, with a lift of his broad shoulders. 'Is Richard such a difficult name to get your prim tongue round? Or Dick will do—the Vice calls me that when he's feeling affable. But not Dickie, I beg of you. Poor Helena used it frequently and, quite frankly, I found it revolting.'

'Oh, hush!' said Elizabeth involuntarily, at the casual, uncomplimentary reference to his late wife. The open windows of the reading-room and the laboratory were not so very far away.

Craske took a pipe from the pocket of his Harris tweed jacket and proceeded to fill it. 'You consider this is a compromising situation even with the fence and the roses?'

'Don't be absurd,' she replied shortly. She could not explain that his mentioning a foible of his dead wife's rather than a virtue sounded discordant and—well, unwise.

'I'd love to compromise you, Elizabeth. But have no fear for the moment—the little beasts are all over at the Oval playing Amazons. When am I going to see you properly?'

'You can come in for tea one day if you like,' she said indifferently.

'And be fallen upon by the gentle cooing Dove? That woman terrifies me. Talking of compromising—all summer she was in and out of my house on some pretext or other. I couldn't get rid of her. She and Mrs Whipple almost fought over the privilege of darning my socks. And the Dean told me later he never gets his darned. He was quite pointed about the matter.'

The Whipples lived on the other side of the Craske house.

That should be a lesson to you not to be such an unscrupulous flirt, thought Elizabeth warmly. She had long ago trained herself to keep at a distance from Richard Craske. Her engagement ring was no protection, especially as Timothy was so often away.

Craske leaned his arms on the low fence. 'Anyway, I can't accept your uncompromising invitation today. Have you forgotten there's a sherry do on at Manning? What a bore beginning of term is! Elizabeth, you're the one bright spot here. How would I get on without you?'

'Quite well,' she replied dryly, pivoting on her heel.

'No, don't go! Actually I wanted to hear about the little Mornane beast. I believe someone buried her sister in your garden last year.'

'Where did you hear that version?'

'Round and about the shop. Does it all mean something or is it, as Gwen Dove would say, but a storm in a tea-cup?'

*It means nothing, and as Miss Dove has already said—least said, soonest mended.'

'For once I applaud the platitudes. Shall I do what I can to squash the rumours?'

Elizabeth looked back at him. 'That would be good of you. It could become an unpleasant business.' She hesitated, then asked slowly, 'You remember the affair, don't you? It happened at the time of—of your wife's accident.'

He knocked the dottle from his pipe and bent down to cover the hot fragments with earth. 'Yes, I remember—rather vaguely.'

Elizabeth tried to see his eyes. 'Do you think there's a chance that Maureen Mornane might not have disappeared voluntarily?'

'Was that the sister's name?' he queried in a careless voice, lifting a rose branch aside. 'I'm afraid I haven't given the problem much thought.'

'She was doing a Science course. What did you think of her?'

'You know I never think of the little beasts unless I have to. I can't even recollect which one she was. All those youngsters seem alike, anyway.'

'Even if they have red hair and a limp?'

'They could be two-headed platinum blondes with cork legs.'

'You mean you didn't know Maureen?'

Craske backed carefully out of the foliage. 'No, I didn't know her,' he replied, now hidden from view.

Slowly and thoughtfully, Elizabeth turned towards the Cottage. She went quietly through the empty lecture room to the laboratory and stood at the window. The fence dividing the Hall property from next door was about twenty feet away, and the garden on both sides was thickly planted with evergreen shrubs. But through a gap between two cotoneasters, she could see several feet of the Craske front path, and a glimpse of the road beyond the picket gate, which was flanked by conifers.

A sound of footsteps aroused her and she went guiltily to the door of the laboratory. 'Is that you, Miss Dove?' The footsteps paused, but there was no reply. She went back to the lecture room. A shabby figure of a man was standing on the other side, his arms held wide. 'Hullo, darling!'

'Timothy!' exclaimed Elizabeth joyfully, rushing forward. 'For a moment I thought you were a tramp.'

'Sorry if I gave you a fright, but I wanted to surprise you. It's heaven to see you again.'

Elizabeth checked her dash across the width of the lecture room. She suddenly recalled she wasn't too pleased with her truant fiancé, and there was something about his appearance that caused more immediate displeasure.

He was tall and lean in a gangling sort of way, with loosely jointed limbs which gave him a resemblance to a flamingo. For a fleeting, unguarded moment she contrasted him with the handsome, well-knit man she had just been speaking with. Their reunion was off to an unpromising start. It was not his present shabby appearance which irked Elizabeth—Timothy was always careless about his clothes—but the shabby untidy beard he had grown.

'Aren't you going to kiss me?' asked Timothy, dropping his arms.

She linked an arm through his, casually affectionate. 'Indeed no—not until you've shaved. Whatever possessed you? All the undergraduates have been growing beards during the vacation.'

Timothy squinted downwards. 'I'm afraid I look a bit of a tramp. No wonder you want to disown me. But I've only just got back and no one seems to know what has happened to my bags. I just had to see you,' he added, with that disarming and intense simplicity which had always proved Elizabeth's undoing.

This time she refused to be weakened.

'Come on into the sitting-room,' she invited brightly, leading the way. 'I can't wait to hear what you've been doing. Did you have a successful trip? Do sit down somewhere.'

He chose Miss Dove's fireside rocker, folded up his flamingo-like legs and regarded his welcoming fiancée warily. 'Yes, most successful, thanks. I was able to locate quite a few members of the Binduk tribe. What I learned from them will be of immense value for my winter trip to the Centre. Is there anything the matter, Elizabeth?' he inquired, after a pause.

'No, of course not,' she replied airily. 'Would you like a glass of sherry or perhaps some sort of snack? I could skip lunch and scrounge something here for the both of us if you like. Or shall we go to the Union?'

'No, don't bother. I've promised to lunch with Father Hopkins. He has very kindly offered to put me up at Manning. I've been asked to do the Moran lecture next month, so what with preparing for that and some research I want to do with the Anthropology Department I should be around for a while. We can lunch together any time.'

'How nice!' said Elizabeth lightly. Then her voice dropped to its customary deep note. She sat down near him. 'Timothy, what about getting married and making the expedition our honeymoon trip? I've always longed to go to the Centre.'

He picked up one of her hands and inspected it idly, 'That's a tempting suggestion, but quite out of the question. These jaunts of mine are no picnic, you know. I wouldn't dream of exposing you to all the discomforts—least of all as a honeymoon trip.' He bent his head swiftly and kissed the soft narrow palm.

Elizabeth snatched her hand away and got up. 'You don't want me to come. You think I'd only be in the way.'

'Yes, you would be,' he said frankly. 'The Centre—the parts I'll be in anyway—is no place for a woman. I'm not running a conducted tour of the sights, Elizabeth.'

'What about the Binduk women? They live there all the year round.'

'Well, as a matter of fact, you're wrong there. The whole tribe migrates farther south during—'

Elizabeth stamped her foot. 'Oh, don't be so pedantic. What I mean is if Binduk women can stand up to the climate and conditions, so can I!'

'Oh, come now, dear. You're being unreasonable. The Binduks have been there for centuries. The women have been bred to the harsh conditions. The thought of your putting up with their way of life—' he looked her up and down dispassionately, then shook his head. 'The idea is simply ludicrous.'

'It's not ludicrous; you just don't want me along. Won't you even give the idea some consideration?'

'The more consideration I give it the more impossible it seems—a delicately nurtured girl like you—'

Elizabeth found herself fingering one of Miss Dove's Dresden figures on the mantelpiece. 'Timothy,' she said dangerously, 'I am a very strong healthy girl. I realize there would be discomforts—plenty of them. I realize too that the expedition would be primarily an anthropology excursion. I promise you I wouldn't be in the way or complain or make demands on your time. All I want is to marry you and share your life, and your interests. I'm tired of marking time here at the University.'

'You're not marking time,' he said soothingly. 'That's another thing—don't think I don't appreciate your intellectual abilities, Elizabeth. I'm not going to ask you to give up your position here to carry my waddies and woomeras, as it were—that's what Binduk girls do, you know. When I come back from the Centre we'll fix some date for the spring. What about that?'

Elizabeth shook her head, 'I want to be married before the winter and go with you.'

His beard jutted forward. Timothy always thrust his jaw out when he was annoyed. 'It's not like you to be so difficult, Elizabeth. When I think of a girl like you with your intellect—'

'Oh, damn my intellect!' she cried. Timothy, I warn you if you don't do as I ask, you might not find me here in the spring.'

His long legs lifted him out of the low chair in extended stages. 'Now, you're just talking nonsense,' he said loftily.

Elizabeth tilted her head to look at him, her dark eyes bright and a most becoming pink warming her camellia-pale skin. 'Am I?' she asked, allowing him to see that she was fiddling with the ruby-set black opal on her left hand. A tense silence fell between them.

A delicate cough sounded. There was a gentle knock at the door and with a little rustle and rattle, Mother Paul glided into the room. 'So sorry to disturb you, Elizabeth, but I have a very special favour to ask of you.' She beamed expectantly at Timothy whose hand went to his beard in a sheepish fashion.

As if he could cover up such a shaggy mane, thought Elizabeth crossly. 'Reverend Mother, may I present my fiancé, Dr Bertram? Our new Warden, Timothy—Mother Raphael has been transferred.'

Mother Paul eyed the offending beard with naïve interest. 'Just like a holy hermit. But whatever do your patients think?'

'Anthropology—not medicine,' he corrected, smiling.

'Oh, then you must be the Dr Bertram who is always poking about obscure parts looking for obscure peoples. One of our Sisters in New Guinea wrote to me about meeting you. She couldn't understand why you found her children—she conducts a native school, Elizabeth—so interesting. As far as she was concerned they were just as trying to teach catechism to as white children. Have you just come back from there, Dr Bertram? How pleased Elizabeth must be to see you!'

Timothy gave his faintly glowering fiancée a sidelong glance. 'Oh, yes—very. Actually I've spent the last few weeks in western New South Wales looking for Binduk tribe stragglers. You must excuse my ruffianly appearance. I only called in for a minute while they were fixing up a room for me at Manning.'

'Then you are intending to stay close at hand for a while? I'm so glad. One really needs the support of an experienced man's advice. And who could be more trustworthy than the man with whom Elizabeth has chosen to share her life? Don't you agree, dear?' she asked the girl fondly.

Timothy eyed the Warden cautiously. He had had some experience of nuns. On past occasions he had frequently found himself doing things for them for which he had neither intention nor inclination.

However, the unenthusiastic murmur from his future helpmeet stung him into offering his advice unequivocally.

'Such trouble we are in!' said Mother Paul, gazing up at him earnestly. 'I daresay Elizabeth hasn't had time to tell you yet, but we very much fear murder has been committed.'

Timothy opened his mouth, rolled an inquiring eye at Elizabeth, then said weakly, 'Oh, now come! Surely you're imagining that!'

'No, indeed. It happened over a year ago now, and it's one of those murders that doesn't look like murder—if you understand what I mean. Everyone seems to consider the girl disappeared of her own accord.'

Elizabeth shelved her personal grievances.

'Maureen Mornane, Tim—you remember the fuss last year. Her sister, Judith, is a freshette here now. She insists Maureen met with foul play. At first I thought she was making some sort of tasteless joke, but Reverend Mother seems to think there might be something in what she says.'

The nun nodded solemnly. 'Such an odd story she poured out to me. I feel I should make some investigation into the matter. What do you suggest, Dr Bertram?'

'The police,' he replied hurriedly and firmly. 'Don't attempt anything of your own accord. The police are the people best qualified to deal with the situation. Send the girl along to them.'

'Oh, I couldn't do that,' said the Warden unhappily. 'She's such a child and quite incoherent when it comes to her sister. I'm very much afraid the police would not pay much heed. Besides,' she turned her gentle gaze from Timothy to Elizabeth and back again, 'I don't think

Judith quite realizes what she has started. It is my belief that there has been more than one murder—and that unless some swift action is taken there may be more.'

5

'Well, someone must be feeling pretty pleased with life,' remarked Miss Dove coyly, picking her way through the curry and rice at lunch.

Elizabeth guessed Miss Dove had learned of Timothy's return, and tried to instil some enthusiasm into her voice. 'Yes, very pleased.' She took a drink of water. Sister Zita had been somewhat prodigal with the curry powder. 'By the way, should anyone inquire for me I won't be in this afternoon. Mother Paul has asked me to chaperon her into town.'

The Science tutor stopped turning over her minced meat as though looking for bacilli and put down her knife and fork. 'Whatever does she want in town? Really, our new Warden seems an extraordinary person! One shouldn't, of course, judge a book by its cover, but I have the gravest fears as to her suitability to the position. Do you know the whole University is alive with rumours concerning our college? And instead of doing something forceful and practical to redeem our position, what does Reverend Mother do? She goes off to town taking a key member of the staff as chaperon.'

Elizabeth shared some of her colleague's exasperation, but Mother Paul had requested her favour so winningly that she had been unable to refuse. 'We won't be away very long. I haven't forgotten that you and I are going to the reception at Manning.'

'Well, I'm due over at the Chemistry school straight after lunch. So Mother Tobias will have to hold the fort here. Why on earth couldn't Reverend Mother have chosen her for this jaunt to town?'

'I wouldn't know,' replied Elizabeth, her eye caught by the students' table as Sister Lydia substituted jam roly-poly for her plate. There seemed to be an unusual air of excitement amongst the girls.

'What are they tittering about now?' asked Miss Dove irritably. 'Is that Mornane girl making trouble again?'

But Judith was eating her lunch quietly, removed from the centre of the disturbance which was, of course, Fiona and her friend Nola.

'That Searle girl's a menace,' muttered Miss Dove. 'I wish to goodness she would marry one of the unfortunate young men she becomes engaged to periodically.'

'I'd rather Fiona than the Markham girl,' voiced Elizabeth, who considered she had more reason to feel ruffled by the morning's frictions than Miss Dove.

'Oh, I agree—absolutely! Of all the priggish little sticky-beaks—hullo, what's that noise?'

A sudden lull fell over the dining-room. Then Fiona cried, 'I believe they're coming now!' She jumped up from her chair and ran to the long windows overlooking the usually quiet Cemetery Road. Several of the others darted after her.

Miss Dove stood up. 'You girls come back and finish your lunch at once. At once—do you hear? Or I'll call Reverend Mother!'

The noise outside had now clarified itself into a kind of chant which came closer every moment. Presently Elizabeth recognized one of the University Commencement songs being intoned by lusty masculine voices.

'It's a rag,' she informed Miss Dove resignedly. 'Margaret Knight warned me the Manning boys were planning one.'

'What a bore youngsters are!' replied Miss Dove, becoming equally fatalistic. 'Shall we stand on our dignity or be disapproving but indulgent onlookers?'

Heather Markham approached the tutor's table. There was a look of exaggerated concern plastered on her pudding face. 'Can't something be done to stop the rag?' she appealed unctuously. 'The good name of Brigid Moore Hall will suffer.'

'Do I understand you to mean they are planning this rag around us here?' demanded Miss Dove, losing her indulgence.

Heather glanced from her to Elizabeth, 'Yes, didn't you know? And it's all because of that dreadful accusation poor Judith Mornane made. Oh, why did she!'

'They're right outside,' reported someone from the windows, with a giggle. 'Don't they look simply terrific? They're supposed to be dressed like girls—couldn't you die! Look Fiona! There's that boy doing Architecture—the one with the fabulous sports car.'

'Where—where? I can't see!'

Miss Dove elbowed her way to the window followed by Elizabeth, with Heather in clinging attendance.

'What an awful din!' declared Monica, in her brusque way. 'They'll all have inflamed tracheas tomorrow.'

'Don't listen too closely to the words, everyone! They might be naughty. They were composed specially for the occasion.'

A voice murmured close to Elizabeth's ear, 'Oh, I'm sorry—I'm sorry! Mother Paul will never forgive me for this.'

Elizabeth turned her head and saw Judith standing near by, her young face woebegone. 'Well, it's no use repining now,' she told her, not unkindly.

The rag had gathered an appreciative audience outside as well as inside the Hall.

'It's disgraceful—just disgraceful!' moaned Heather, as she enjoyed the spectacle. 'We'll never live this down.'

Fiona gave an impatient glance over her shoulder. 'Oh, rubbish! Who takes it seriously? Stop pretending you don't think it's fun. Golly! I do believe they are coming in. Silly muggins—I bet they'll get gated for this.'

A group of about a dozen male students, all in various stages of female dress and undress, crowded through the gate, cheered on by their less intrepid supporters.

'This is getting beyond a laughing matter,' snapped Miss Dove, as the supporters, hanging over the fence, began pelting flour at the principals to urge them on. 'Where is the Warden?'

One undergraduate in the centre of the group was being pushed and pulled up to the front door. Under a tattered college gown he was wearing a skimpy floral dress, which displayed two lengths of muscular hairy legs ending in the ludicrous torture of high-heeled shoes. His face was ridiculously made-up and tied about with a scarf, from which appeared a bushy frizz of bright red hair.

'What on earth's the matter with his face? Looks like he has the measles.'

'Freckles, dope! He's supposed to be—'

'Oh, hush!' warned Heather, pointing to Judith. 'What an extraordinary get-up! But I can't help thinking—'

'Let's get out!' someone cried suddenly, and they all pushed into the hall.

Elizabeth was swept along with Heather still clinging to her, while Miss Dove could be heard expostulating, 'Empty vessels make the most sound! Will you girls come to order at once, please!'

Then another sudden lull fell on the students and those still in the dining-room tried to see what was holding them back. 'What's going on now? Let us get through!'

The Warden, with Mother Tobias looking ready for martyrdom at the hands of revolutionaries behind her, was standing in the hall watching them gravely. She did not speak until the door-bell rang. Then, withdrawing one of her hands which had been folded under her scapular, she motioned towards the door.

'Would someone kindly open it, please?'

Miss Dove raised her voice over the heads indignantly. 'Reverend Mother, it's just an outrageous prank by some students from Manning College.'

'Open the door,' repeated the nun, 'Miss Drew!' Elizabeth went forward reluctantly. The male student in the red wig stood revealed on the threshold. When he saw the gathering of women, in the centre of which were two nuns, he looked even more foolish than his absurd attire warranted.

'Who are you?' asked the Warden serenely, without moving. 'What do you want?'

'I'm Maureen Mornane!' squeaked the unfortunate buffoon, pricked on by his companions. 'I've come back! Ugh!' A flour 'bomb' hit him between the shoulder-blades and scattered on the chaste parquetry.

There were one or two nervous giggles from the girls and a stifled sob from Judith Mornane. The Warden was silent for several seconds. She surveyed the figure on the doorstep from top to toe dispassionately.

Then she addressed the impersonator. 'You may return to your college now. Elizabeth, close the door!'

Without another word she turned and, closely followed by Mother Tobias, retired to the nuns' quarters in the back of the house.

The girls drifted back to the remains of their lunch. A few, with less sensibility than the others, watched the retreat of the rag through the windows. One of the onlookers, unaware of the crushing reception at the front door, had seized a hose from the garden and was merrily dousing the principal performers.

Presently the procession moved away, and a strange and gloomy silence fell over Brigid Moore Hall once more.

Elizabeth felt so keenly for the Warden after this further affliction, that she resolved to act the part of chaperon with as much cheerfulness as she could muster.

However, it was only when Mother Paul, cloaked and gloved, was safely in the back seat of Elizabeth's secondhand Holden that the precise nature of paying a little call in the city was revealed.

'So good of you, dear child,' declared the Warden, avoiding the girl's eyes in the rear vision mirror as she disentangled her large cotton umbrella from her rosary beads. 'I didn't like to ask Mother Tobias. I couldn't help feeling she might not care for the trip. Such a temptation to disobedience, especially as I'm sure I am already a severe strain on her charity. And she was so forbearing over that unpleasant business at lunch.'

Elizabeth, waiting at the end of Cemetery Road for a clearance in the traffic, tried to catch her eye. 'Where are we going, Mother Paul?'

'Now, Elizabeth! Before that big lorry comes.'

The girl swung into Sydney Road obediently. 'Why wouldn't Mother Tobias care for the trip?' she asked uneasily.

'Well, I can't actually vouch for her dislike, but I felt sure you wouldn't dislike it quite as much,' replied the Warden naively. 'We are going to pay a little visit to the police—at Russell Street Headquarters, you know. I think it is that tall, pinkish building over to the left with the wireless mast—just like a finger of warning to wrongdoers, don't you agree, dear?'

Elizabeth drove on in silence, but with several grim and pithy remarks forming themselves in her mind. They were nearing the city now, not a propitious time for argument or protestation.

'Such sound advice from that young man you are going to marry,' the Warden chattered on. 'Though, to be sure, I had already resolved on going to the police. Being a religious does hamper one, if you know what I mean.'

Does it? thought Elizabeth grimly, turning into Russell Street. A craven and cunning means of escape presented itself. 'I don't know where I'll be able to park the car, Mother Paul. Will it be all right to drop you and then call back later?'

'But there's a great empty space right in front of the building,' the nun pointed out. 'Draw in now, dear.'

'I rather think that is reserved for police cars.'

'Never mind. I'll inquire from that officer standing outside the door if we can leave the car for a short while. They are always so kind and considerate.'

As soon as Elizabeth drew into the kerb, the policeman approached with chiding brows asking quite clearly, 'And just what do you think you're doing?'

Mother Paul extricated herself from the back seat, advanced on him with candid eyes and spoke a few soft appealing words.

'There now!' she exclaimed, returning in triumph. 'He says you may leave the car after all.'

Avoiding the policeman's bemused eye, Elizabeth followed the Warden up the steps and through the swing doors. Not since she stumbled on the dais going up for her degree in Wilson Hall had she felt so self-conscious. The neat young policewoman, past whose inquiry desk many startling characters had passed, seemed visibly moved at the appearance of a nun.

'I wish to see the officer in charge of missing persons,' requested Mother Paul.

Taking a noticeable grip of herself, the policewoman requested their names and addresses, filled in a card with rather less than her usual efficiency, and stumbled in her verbal directions to the Missing Persons Bureau.

The Warden and Elizabeth went up in the lift with several tough-faced brawny-bodied young men with hats worn low over their foreheads, the formidableness of whose mien seemed to melt away as they all jostled to remove their hats. It took their combined efforts to open the door when the lift came to rest.

'Always so helpful and courteous,' murmured Mother Paul, as they were left in a long, bare corridor.

Unfortunately, the officer in charge of the Missing Persons Bureau was less favourably impressed by the presence of a nun at Russell

Street Police Headquarters. He treated them politely enough, but Elizabeth had the impression that he regarded the Warden as an eccentric. She did not blame him for this in the least.

When Mother Paul, without preamble, requested to see the report on Maureen Mornane's disappearance, saying that she had grounds for feeling dissatisfied with the general suggestion that she was in hiding by her own choice, he made no attempt to select any of the bulky folders filed in the shelves about him. Instead, he asked for the precise nature of that dissatisfaction of Sister's.

'I regret I cannot be precise — yet,' returned Mother Paul candidly. 'But there are one or two odd matters which I feel sure mean something in regard to Maureen. If only I knew how far the police investigation went, I could continue from there and the odd matters might become less peculiar.'

The officer shot a glance at Elizabeth, as though to determine if he had two lunatics with whom to deal. Then he said to the nun. 'I'm sorry. Sister, but until you have definite information to lay I cannot disclose what is in our report.'

He got up to close the interview, expecting Mother Paul to do the same. But she sat with her black-gloved hands clasped round her umbrella, deep in thought.

'Who was in charge of the inquiries into Maureen Mornane's disappearance?' she asked.

This time the glance at Elizabeth was somewhat testy. He plainly expected her to help rid him of his troublesome visitor. When she too remained seated, though with rather a heightened colour, he gave an impatient mutter, strode over to one of the shelves and pulled out a file.

'The case came under Inspector Savage's direction,' he told them, after glancing at the contents. 'The actual inquiries were handled by one of his detectives.'

The nun rose, 'I would like to see Inspector Savage,' she announced simply. 'Would you be so kind as to direct us where to go?'

In a goaded voice, the officer told them the way to the Criminal Investigation Branch.

Mother Paul thanked him gravely, then added, 'Shall I take that file with me? I promise you most faithfully not to peep, and it will save Inspector Savage having to send up for it.'

'If you don't mind. I'd rather wait until he does send for it,' was the strained reply. He ushered them out of his office, then made a dive for the intercommunication telephone.

6

Elizabeth suspected that Inspector Savage would have been warned of his unusual visitors, and was fully prepared for the humiliation of being fobbed off again. She was rather surprised when they entered a small bare room on the ground floor to be greeted with more than a polite disinterest.

'Reverend Mother Mary St Paul of the Cross?' He held out one hand as he intoned her full name with a solemnity at variance with the gleam of humour in his eyes. 'I once heard a colleague of mine speak of you. Weren't you in charge of that girls' hostel from which a drug ring was operating?'

The nun shook his hand, saying gratefully but guiltily, 'Such a shocking way in which to have one's credentials vouched for, but perhaps just as well. Do you know, Elizabeth, I can't help thinking that good conscientious man with all the files upstairs considered there was something odd about us? This is Miss Drew, Inspector, from Brigid Moore Hall at the University. She is one of the staff your detectives questioned about a student's disappearance last year.'

'How do you do, Miss Drew? I understand it is in connexion with the missing student that you wish to see me. Reverend Mother. Please sit down and tell me what you are worried about.'

He placed chairs for them and then sat down leisurely behind his desk. Elizabeth felt at ease for the first time since they had entered the building.

'My worry,' said the nun, sighing a little, 'is murder!'

Savage's face remained expressionless. 'You suspect that the missing student has been murdered?'

Mother Paul inclined her head, but there was an apologetic note in her voice. 'I do trust you are a patient man, Inspector, because I know from books how detectives dislike feminine fancies. Let me confess at once that I have nothing to substantiate my suspicions—in fact, the notions I have seem odd even to me. Perhaps if I were to tell you what has happened since I became Warden of the college only a few days ago?'

'Please do,' he invited, leaning back in an attitude of being ready to listen all day.

Mother Paul embarked on her story, relating Judith Mornane's accusation in the students' recreation room, the conversation she had had with the girl and the discussion between Elizabeth and Miss Dove.

'My Science tutor's suggestion that Maureen could have panicked after finding Mrs Helena Craske's body in the bath is incredible, Inspector. But, as Miss Drew pointed out, why should the child have stayed away all this time? Furthermore, it seems reasonable to suppose that if the discovery of a dead body was the only cause of her fear, she would have fled to her family. Now here is one of my odd notions,' she added hesitantly.

Savage nodded encouragement. 'Please go on.'

'Supposing Maureen Mornane saw not merely a dead body, but Mrs Craske in the process of drowning! Supposing she saw someone actually holding the unfortunate woman under the water!'

'Mother Paul!' whispered Elizabeth, aghast.

The nun pressed her hand. 'I know, dear—very dreadful! But for poor Maureen I wouldn't have entertained the notion—especially as I understand the official verdict on Mrs Craske's death was accidental drowning.'

'You are suggesting,' said Savage, without emotion, 'that Maureen was a witness to murder and that as a result she is either hiding in fear of her life or was also murdered for knowing too much?'

The nun replied earnestly, 'Yes, that is my suggestion, but I am far from being satisfied with it. There are one or two matters that just don't seem to fit properly.'

'And they are?' prompted Savage, as the Warden hesitated again.

'One is the change in Maureen's behaviour which took place before Mrs Craske's death.' She stressed the last four words in a puzzled voice. 'According to such evidence as I have been able to glean, this change in Maureen occurred on her arrival at Brigid Moore Hall. Could she have learned in advance of a plan to murder Mrs Craske and gone to the Craske home three days later in order to do what she could to stop it? She was a high-spirited, courageous girl, but I can't believe that a love of adventure alone would have prevented her from divulging her suspicions of a murder plan to some authoritative person. Of course, she may have considered that no one would believe her, and yet—' her voice took on a note of vexation. 'I can't imagine any murderer who has been clever enough to get away with the crime for as long as this being so stupid as to allow anyone to learn of the murder plan in advance. What do you think, Inspector?'

He was frowning heavily, as though turning matters over in his mind. There was silence in the little bare room, save for the ticking of an incongruous-looking alarm clock standing on the window sill. Presently, with the heavy frown making the lines of his face grim instead of humorous, the inspector sat forward and took up the telephone on his desk.

'This is Savage speaking. I want the Missing Persons file on Maureen Mornane—the eighteen-year-old girl who disappeared twelve months ago. And would you see what we have on a Mrs Helena Craske—an inquest was held on her about the same time.'

He put down the receiver, his eyes on the nun's smooth, guileless countenance.

'Believe me, Mother Paul, Maureen Mornane's case has never been considered closed—any more than the many other cases of missing persons in our records. They all come up again and again for investigation.'

'Then you will reopen the investigation at once?' she inquired, with confidence. 'Thank you, Inspector—we are most grateful.'

He smiled at the simple appreciation. 'It is we who should be grateful. The theory that Maureen met with foul play was considered, but nothing could be found to back up the premise. The girl had a happy home life—there was no question of any—er—romantic entanglements—she had just arrived at the University without time to make even the slightest enemy, and she was leading a protected life at Brigid Moore Hall. As you can see, there was simply no lead at all to follow up.'

The Warden assured him earnestly, 'One cannot proceed on premise alone.'

'The first and only motive for Maureen's possible murder has been made today,' Savage went on. 'But even supposing that motive has some foundation, the mystery still remains the same. Where—dead or alive—is Maureen Mornane?'

The girl and the nun merely looked back at him, the one with blank incomprehension, the other rather absently, as though engaged with her own speculations.

'Miss Drew, why were my men not informed that Maureen was last seen apparently leaving Richard Craske's house?'

Elizabeth started at the sudden question. 'Miss Dove did not mention that possibility of having seen Maureen until after the inquiries had died down.'

A knock at the door took Savage's attention from her. A young man came in and placed two folders on the desk. There was a note clipped to one which the inspector read with a twitch to his mouth, crumpled and put into his pocket with an involuntary glance at the nun.

Elizabeth hoped that his colleague's comments on the contentious file would keep him diverted. But instead, he opened the other folder first, gave it a swift perusal, then remarked with a casualness she found ominous, 'I see Professor Craske's whereabouts at the time of his wife's death were clearly established—vouched for by Miss Dove herself and a Dean of one of the Faculties, Professor Edward Whipple.'

'Is the husband always the obvious and mundane suspect?' asked Elizabeth boldly.

'Yes, that is so,' he agreed, raising his eyes to meet hers. 'Especially if there is money involved or other—er—romantic interests.'

Elizabeth gave Mother Paul a sidelong glance, but she still appeared deep in her own thoughts. 'Mrs Craske had no money to my knowledge. As for the—the other matter, there was no indication that the Craskes were not an ordinary married couple.'

His lack of comment seemed to indicate scepticism, and he said presently, as though bringing his list of the obvious up to date, 'I see Mrs Craske was something of an invalid. Her state of health was taken into account in the post mortem report. It appears she had been under medical advice for a nervous condition for a long time.'

Mother Paul raised her head suddenly. 'Isn't that rather an ambiguous diagnosis?'

The inspector nodded. 'Yes, it could mean that the lady was something of a hypochondriac. There is a report here from her private physician—"complaints of insomnia, migraine, lack of appetite and general debility." For years she had been receiving all the usual treatment—tranquillizers, vitamin injections, etc.—without improvement. With that type of woman there is, of course, always the chance of suicide, but apparently nothing could be found to back up the theory.'

'Would the same chance apply to murder?' asked the nun.

'Yes, any one of three things could have happened to Mrs Craske,' he replied quietly. 'Accident, suicide, murder. It all depended on the circumstantial evidence available at the time.'

He turned over a few papers, then pushed the file away to open the second one. 'We'll leave Mrs Craske for the moment and turn to Maureen Mornane.

'According to this report Maureen left her home on the morning of March the fifteenth and was driven to the nearest railway station—a small town in the Wimmera district called Mulgoa—by her father and younger sister Judith. The railway line is a branch one which necessitates changing trains at a junction half-way to Melbourne. Maureen's plan was to spend the night of the fifteenth with relatives who lived some miles out of the town, but as her train was late in arriving at Ararat, she rang them to say she would spend the night at a hotel instead. No objection was raised to this suggestion as the hotel was kept by friends of the relatives, who reported Maureen as being in high spirits. She spoke of a letter she had written to her family back at Mulgoa.

'On the morning of the sixteenth she said good-bye to the hotel people, went back to the station and caught the train to Melbourne. She arrived at Brigid Moore Hall in the afternoon, unpacked her bags in the room allotted to her, made arrangements about the course she intended taking, and, in general, became merged into college life. But on the morning of March the twentieth she disappeared from the University, having been last seen at breakfast time in the dining-room of Brigid Moore Hall.

'Until now, that was the last information we had of Maureen's movements,' added Savage, looking up again. 'Here is a description of her appearance—red hair, slight build, limp, etc., the clothes she was wearing and a photograph.'

'May I see it?' asked Mother Paul.

He passed it across the desk. 'Rather a poor one, I'm afraid. They always are—and invariably several years old. We had it blown up, of course, but the process rather tends to disfigure it further. And here is the letter she wrote.'

Mother Paul passed the photograph on to Elizabeth and took the sheet of cardboard to which Maureen's letter and its envelope had been pasted so as to preserve them. With a feeling of great sadness she read:

Darling folks at home.

You'll probably think me quite mad writing when I have only just left you, but this stupid train is so slow and makes so many stops I just have to fill in the time somehow. Why does one always feel chatty on one's own and not when one is in a crowd? I feel I could write reams, but I daresay the mood will give out after a couple of pages, so don't be alarmed!

It's just fabulous knowing I'm on my way to the 'Varsity. I can hardly believe it's true about the scholarship. Wouldn't it be ghastly if a mistake had been made and some other girl . . .

And so it went on—redundant outpourings which gave the nun a mental picture of a happy, carefree girl looking forward to an unmarred future that only youth can visualize.

About the middle of the third page, Maureen's mood must have evaporated. The last sentences were short and forced. She had finished the letter with—*'I'll write more later. I'll know all about Brigid Moore Hall and the University. Tons of love for the present.'*

Mother Paul turned her attention to the envelope. 'Mailed at a box in the University grounds on the evening of the sixteenth,' said Savage, who had been watching her.

The nun passed the card back. 'I wonder why she didn't continue it. So odd when she obviously intended giving her impressions of the University.'

'She probably got into a crowd and didn't feel chatty,' the Inspector replied, underlining the sentence with a forefinger. 'She did send a telegram stating she had arrived safely. Here it is—

Arrived safely. B.M. terrific. Writing again.

'Well, she still seemed happy when she sent the telegram,' replied the nun. 'The evening of the sixteenth—the day before the University opened. When did the change in her demeanour occur, I wonder?'

'I spoke to Maureen that evening,' interposed Elizabeth. 'There was no difference in her demeanour the next two days that I observed.'

'To Miss Drew, Maureen seemed a shy, unobtrusive normal freshette, Inspector.'

'Hardly normal,' corrected Elizabeth absently, squinting at the photograph in an endeavour to discover some familiar memory in the picture face.

The Warden turned on her. 'What do you mean, Elizabeth?'

Elizabeth looked startled. 'Go on, Miss Drew,' urged Savage quietly.

'I don't know why I said that,' the girl stammered. 'It's just—well, Maureen was too unobtrusive. The police report that you just read said something about her becoming merged into college life, but it seems to me now that she deliberately kept to herself and made no attempt to enter into college life.'

There was a pause which was broken by a soft remark from Mother Paul. 'How odd for one who considered Brigid Moore Hall— what was the word used? Ah yes—terrific! Such a uniformity about adjectives nowadays.'

The inspector regarded her keenly. Unlike Elizabeth, he seemed to pay attention to the Warden's irrelevancies. 'Are you implying that Maureen deceived her family into thinking all was well when there was something seriously wrong? That could be the reason for her not adding to the letter. They would have spotted it in a letter, but not in the brevity of a telegram.'

'Yes, the telegram would have deceived them,' agreed the nun.

Savage's gaze grew more concentrated. There was something in the limpid eyes which looked back at him that almost tempted him to ask what strange notions was Mother Paul entertaining now. He felt a pang of understanding for his colleague in the Missing Persons Bureau, and wondered if he were not making a mistake in judgement by paying such close attention. This unusual woman, a mixture of shrewdness and naïveness, was, after all, a recluse from the world. While he had no doubt that human weakness displayed itself on occasions even in religious community life, she could not possibly know the extent of propensity to evil. Yet here she was calmly, though admittedly with regret, maintaining that not one but two murders had been committed — and at the University of all places.

But Mother Paul disarmed his misgivings. 'I can't tell you how grateful I am for your sympathetic hearing, Inspector. Or what a relief it is to relinquish such terrible responsibilities to the right quarter.'

He smiled warmly. 'You did very well to come, and I promise that everything will be done to investigate your suspicions.'

She smiled at him trustfully, then became serious. 'If murder was done a year ago, some wicked person is feeling very triumphant at having accomplished it without arousing suspicion. Even now, with rumours circulating around the University, there must still be a sense of security — first, because of the facetious way in which the rumours are being treated, and, secondly, having been successful so far there is the incentive to keep on should the necessity arise.' The Warden's eyes grew troubled as she added. 'That is what I am afraid of, Inspector — another murder.'

He nodded briefly. 'Yes, murderers become drunk with a sense of their own power and astuteness.'

He turned towards Elizabeth. 'Miss Drew, is there anything — anything at all you remember now that may have been the cause of Maureen Mornane's abnormal behaviour? As Mother Paul pointed out, this change occurred before Mrs Craske's death. Think hard, Miss Drew! Could Maureen have recognized someone or something at your college which would be the reason for her keeping out of the way?'

Elizabeth closed her eyes. Strange how she could only visualize Judith when she tried to recall the elder sister. 'I'm sorry — I can think of nothing.'

'Keep trying, Miss Drew,' advised Savage. And if you should remember anything I'll give Mother Paul instructions how to get in touch with me.'

'I'll do my best,' the girl promised.

He addressed the nun again. 'Perhaps if you could get some of the students who were associated with Maureen to do the same? There is a chance one of them might recall something she did or said that will give us a lead.'

The Warden nodded and glanced at Elizabeth. 'That humourless child who has such good intentions—the one taking Social Studies. What is her name again, Elizabeth?'

'Heather Markham?' queried Elizabeth doubtfully. 'Yes, she might be able to help. I understand it was not from want of trying that Heather was unable to break through Maureen's reserve.'

Inspector Savage then wound up the interview with a word of warning. 'I need hardly stress the need for both caution and discretion at this juncture—both for your own sakes and for the success of police investigations. Furthermore, although your suspicions are justified and reasonable, there is always the chance that you might be—'

'Barking up the wrong tree?' supplied Mother Paul helpfully, as he searched for a mild phrase.

He looked taken aback, then laughed. 'Yes, that's about it.' He rose, came round his desk and opened the door for them. 'I'll be in touch with you in a day or two,' he promised, as they said good-bye and left.

But Mother Paul and Elizabeth were to see him sooner than that. By the time they arrived back at Brigid Moore Hall, a second student had disappeared.

7

A light repast of tea, sandwiches and cake was always laid out in the dining-room of Brigid Moore Hall late afternoon so that anyone who wished could come in between lectures and help themselves. Elizabeth slipped in for a quick cup of tea before changing to attend the reception at Manning College. It was her intention if Heather Markham was there to draw her aside and get her to talk about Maureen. When she saw that the girl was absent, she merely made a mental note to seek her out after supper.

The party at Manning was one of a series of informal gatherings which took place at the beginning of the year at the various colleges. It was another warm day, and Elizabeth wore a white dress trimmed with guipure lace and a most becoming red straw hat. Miss Dove, who eyed its pertness with a touch of envy, had on the navy blue morocain two-piece in which she declared she always felt right.

'And to where did you and the Warden flit off this afternoon?' she inquired, as they crossed Cemetery Road and entered the north gates of the University grounds.

'Just a business call in the city,' the girl replied, with new-found guardedness.

'The Warden would have been better employed doing something about business at home. Is she not going to take any stand about that disgraceful affair at lunchtime?'

'What can Reverend Mother do other than ignore it?' countered Elizabeth, nettled by the cross-examination.

'Well, I'm always one to let bygones be bygones,' declared the other briskly, 'but we'll see in what light the Rector views the rag.'

Manning College was a gothic-styled building, its mellow exterior clung about with creeping ivy which here and there showed the first vivid signs of autumn. The two cool dim parlours in the front of the house were filled with academic-looking men attached to unlikely-looking women wearing the same flowered toques that would appear in the reception rooms of the other colleges during the next two weeks.

The only uncovered feminine head belonged to Manning's housekeeper, Margaret Knight, who, neat and efficient in black, was pouring tea at an extempore buffet set up at the back of the mosaic-laid hall.

The Rector was tall and ascetic-looking, but with easy and cheerful manners which made him a popular figure. He was known to have a profound intellect, unerring powers of theological debate, some athletic prowess and the best collection of classic jazz records in the state. The college under his guidance had earned a reputation for brilliant graduates.

He greeted the two representatives from Brigid Moore Hall jocularly, inquired after the new Warden, made an ecclesiastical quip or two and then sent them to mingle with the rest of the guests.

After a slow tour of the rooms, Elizabeth allowed herself to be summoned by the imperious beckoning finger of the wife of one of the Deans.

'The very gal I wanted to see!' announced Mrs Whipple, in her brassy voice. 'What's all this I hear about your college? Eddie, find another plate of those meringue things, will you?'

Elizabeth smiled at the Dean, whose imperturbability tinged with irony always made her wonder if he consciously modelled himself on Mr Bennet. Mrs Whipple was an exuberant, buxom woman rather like a one-time music-hall queen. She always wore straining lace fronts to her dresses, dead white face-powder, a henna-coloured hair fringe and an aura of violent perfume. It was generally supposed that the Dean had made an irrevocable mistake in his rash, hotheaded youth, when students did things like marrying the local barmaid.

'And what have you heard about Brigid Moore?' asked Elizabeth carefully.

'Some rigmarole about that girl who vanished last year having been murdered. Is there any truth in it?'

Elizabeth forced a laugh. 'I shouldn't think so. You know what a place this is for rumour.'

'Lor' love us, yes!' agreed Mrs Whipple, rolling her eyes as though to beguile the gallery. 'I was only telling Dick Craske it's about time he got married again. Otherwise people will start having doubts.'

'Doubts? What sort of doubts?'

Mrs Whipple drooped a mascara-beaded eyelash. 'You know what

I mean. It's not right a fine, healthy man like Dick—not that Helena could have been much chop, always drooping around taking pills and reading poetry. That's not what a man wants. He needs—'

'Oh, yes,' interrupted Elizabeth hastily. 'I see what you mean.'

'What else could I mean? I thought gals nowadays knew all the answers and a bit more too.'

'Would you like a cup of tea or a glass of sherry, Elizabeth?' asked a familiar and welcome voice. 'I see you're fixed up, Mrs Whipple.'

Elizabeth turned gratefully. 'Oh, Timothy! Sherry will do, thanks. But I'll come with you. Mrs Whipple will excuse us, I know.'

Mrs Whipple brushed her lace front clear of meringue crumbs. 'That's right, dears! I know you want to be off somewhere to hold hands. Eddie and I were the same before we got married.' She gave a lusty, throaty chuckle and another wink.

They moved away, and Timothy said cheerfully. 'What a dreadful woman!'

Elizabeth paused to admire the immense floral display of tawny chrysanthemums on the mantelpiece.

'I'll wait here while you get the sherry.'

'Well, don't get caught up again, will you? I feel I've hardly seen you.'

'I won't,' she promised. She watched his long spare figure slip easily through the crowds. He had on the grey suit she had made him buy in the spring. It made him look more substantial, and less as though one dimension were missing. The thought that he may have taken care over his appearance especially made her smile indulgently, and she suddenly realized that the offensive beard had been removed.

Her softened gaze was caught by Professor Craske who was staring at her with faintly raised brows from the other side of the room. He had made no attempt to come near her. Miss Dove fluttered in his vicinity like a moth attracted by a strong light. She was by no means the only woman who seemed to be trying to attract his attention, but she was the most obvious.

Elizabeth felt her face stiffen. She felt an angry impulse to shatter his charming aplomb and imagined herself crossing the room to say, 'Oh, by the way, Richard, do you know the police are looking into your wife's death again? They think she might have been murdered.

Just as well Gwen Dove has given you an alibi.'

A glass was put into her hand. 'Here you are, darling! Genuine old Spanish dry, so Father Hopkins declares. One of his confrères, who was chaplain on the last pilgrimage, brought it in under his cassock. Here's to us!'

She tilted her face, smiling with an extra warmth that, for some reason, she wanted Craske to witness. 'Timothy! You've shaved off your beard. And it must have been the envy of all Manning.'

He ran his hand over his cheeks and chin. 'I must admit I felt a pang parting with it, but I couldn't have you thinking I looked a tramp.' He paused, regarding her with simple intentness. 'You do look lovely, Elizabeth.'

She felt a glow, but said mockingly. 'What? Am I better looking than a Binduk woman?'

'Are you still cross about the Centre trip? Seeing you now convinces me even more of the impracticability of your coming too.'

'Well, I didn't intend taking this frock or these shoes,' she answered dryly, showing him one pencil-heeled scarlet shoe.

He glanced down absently, then asked abruptly, 'What on earth's that new Warden of yours up to?'

She sipped her sherry. 'She's been taking your advice. She thinks you are a nice young man.'

He looked uneasy. 'What advice did I give her?' Elizabeth lowered her voice. 'To go to the police with Judith Mornane's suggestion that her sister was probably murdered.

His uneasiness developed into alarm. 'The police must have thought you a pair of cranks.'

'No, indeed! A very nice inspector called Savage has promised to look further into Maureen's disappearance and—and another matter.' She could not help a glance in Craske's direction but he was no longer in the room.

'Well, that sounds like a gentle brush-off,' Timothy remarked confidently. 'Your nice inspector must have had dealings with cranks before.'

Miss Dove came up to join them. 'How do you do, Dr Bertram? It's nice to see the wanderer's return.'

'Are you wanting to leave now?' asked Elizabeth.

'I think having put in an appearance, we may now retire grace-fully. I've got some stuff to prepare before supper, so duty calls!'

'Must you go?' muttered Timothy. 'I still haven't seen you properly.'

'It's a situation that could be easily rectified,' returned Elizabeth pointedly. 'But just now I'm a working girl doing a job which you said wouldn't be fair to ask me to give up — remember?'

She left him searching hopelessly for a way to deny his words, and caught up with Miss Dove, who cast a sidelong glance at her colleague's pinkened face and bright eyes.

'Faint heart never won a fair lady,' she remarked cryptically. 'Hullo, there's Margaret! We'd better stop and speak to her. It doesn't do to neglect the lower orders.'

Richard Craske was leaning up against the buffet with a cup of tea in his hand. On the other side Miss Knight, lips compressed as though there was a sour taste in her mouth, was piling up empty plates with a rapid efficiency. However, she looked as though she was enjoying being disapproving of whatever Craske was saying to her.

'Good evening, Margaret!' said Miss Dove heartily, as they came up. 'Still hard at doing the honours? It has been a most successful and enjoyable party. Ah, Professor Craske! Are you also leaving now? Perhaps we can all walk back together.'

He drained his tea, threw Elizabeth a glance of droll resignation and gave Margaret his cup and saucer with a word of thanks. 'That would be very pleasant,' he replied mockingly.

Miss Knight put a hand on Elizabeth's white-gloved arm. 'Just a minute, Miss Drew.'

Elizabeth turned back. 'What is it, Margaret?'

'About the rag! Perhaps I should have told the Rector. Did it cause much fuss? Was the Warden upset?'

'Not unduly.'

Margaret dabbed vigorously at some spilt tea, and swept a few crumbs into the palm of her hand. 'I'm glad to know it, I'm sure. Though I heard quite a different story, if you'll pardon me contra-dicting you.'

'You listen to too many rumours,' said Elizabeth coldly.

'This wasn't a rumour. It was straight from the horse's mouth.

That fat girl doing Social Studies rang up to complain to the Rector. She said the Hall was in terrible turmoil.'

Oh, damn Heather, thought Elizabeth. Just the interfering thing she would do! Aloud she said, 'I'm sure the Rector would not pay much attention to a student's complaints.'

The housekeeper's eyes gleamed. 'Too right he wouldn't! You don't think I'd let a little busybody like her speak to the Rector! 'This is Heather Markham from Brigid Moore Hall,' she says, ever so grand. 'I wish to speak to Reverend Father Hopkins, please.' Well, she spoke to Margaret Knight instead. And what an ear-basher! You can imagine how busy I was with this party on this afternoon and Christies not sending enough cakes so that someone had to dash out for more—yours truly, naturally. No one can realize the work and organization I put into a show like this, least of all the brainy big-wigs who come to guzzle.'

Elizabeth broke in on the familiar recital. 'You did well not to bother the Rector.'

Margaret seemed gratified. She dropped tea spoons into an empty milk jug and poured in hot water from the urn. 'I've got some brains, though you mightn't think it. "See that the Rector is informed, please Margaret" says Miss Grand Manners—the cheek of her! Well, that's all I wanted to tell you, Miss Drew. You'd better go and see what you can do about taking Miss Busybody Markham down a peg or two while I see about washing these dishes.'

But the Rector stopped Elizabeth before she reached the front door. He was always an adroit host. 'Are you leaving? So good of you to come! You must be glad Tim Bertram is making a temporary sojourn here. We're delighted to have him, of course—a splendid fellow! But I don't have to ask you to agree to that, do I? Ha! Ha! Tell your Reverend Mother I'll drop in some time for a visit.'

'She'll be pleased to see you and thank you for the hospitality, Father. It has been a pleasant gathering.'

'Good, good! By the way,' his sunken eyes danced with sudden merriment. 'Tell your Warden that a few of my lads are coming over at the week-end to do any odd jobs she might care to line up—gardening, wood-chopping and suchlike.'

Elizabeth's eyes twinkled. The Rector had heard of the rag and was taking his own inimitable disciplinary measures. 'Mother Paul will appreciate both your motive and your offer,' she told him, and said good-bye.

'So that's why young Baynes was weeding our garden this afternoon,' said Miss Dove, applying generous daubs of mayonnaise to her supper salad. 'He was the one in the red wig who came to the door. The Rector must have caught them sneaking back to Manning and lost no time in passing sentence.'

'Odd—Father Hopkins said the week-end.' Elizabeth frowned. 'Baynes? Isn't that the boy who used to visit Helena Craske?'

Miss Dove laughed shortly. 'Did you know he left off being a poet when she died? No one to listen to his weird and wonderful verse, I daresay. Now he's changed from taking himself seriously to making a nuisance of himself. May I trouble you for the bread?'

Elizabeth passed the plate slowly.

'Where's our social worker?' Fiona Searle's lilting voice demanded, over the subdued talk of the students' table.

Elizabeth looked up suddenly, running her eyes down the two rows until they met the empty place. 'Did Heather Markham have a pass to go out?' she asked Miss Dove in an undertone.

'She didn't get one from me. Perhaps she didn't hear the bell.' Miss Dove raised her voice. 'One of you girls—Monica will do—run over to the Cottage and tell Heather no one is allowed to miss meals at Brigid Moore. She's probably in the reading-room.'

Monica scraped her chair back and went out, nibbling at a piece of lettuce in her hand.

'Heather wasn't there when I came back from Manning,' said Elizabeth quietly. 'And I heard the supper bell from the Cottage.'

'Then I daresay she's in her room.'

Elizabeth got up quickly. 'I'll go and see. Don't let the girls panic.'

The Science tutor looked at her blankly. 'What's there to panic about?'

The girl moved away without replying, smiling brightly at the curious faces now turned towards her. Judith Mornane caught her eye for a moment, and Elizabeth's heart missed a beat as she thought—Inspector Savage wanted us to speak to Heather, to find out if she knew anything about Maureen.

Fiona was seated at the end of the table near the door. Elizabeth bent down to her ear. 'Be a good girl and start some table game or other.'

After a swift searching glance, the girl nodded her fair head, and at once began intoning in a droll sing-song voice. 'The ship travelling to South America was carrying a cargo of apples, artichokes, antelopes—'

Elizabeth closed the door quickly behind her, then darted for the stairs.

Each student at Brigid Moore had her own room, furnished as a combined bedroom and study. Cards bearing their names were fitted into brass holders on the doors.

Elizabeth inspected them rapidly, then knocked and entered Heather Markham's room. It was empty, silent and orderly, but for a satchel and gown thrown on the bed and some scattered sheets of paper on the floor that the curtains at the open window had brushed from the desk.

Elizabeth stooped and picked them up. Her eye was caught by the words—'Dearest Daddy, I have been neglecting you shamefully—' Heather had been writing a letter home. She anchored the papers under a book and went out into the passage. 'Heather!' she called, and made a swift inspection of the bathrooms. But there was no sign of anyone and she went back downstairs.

Monica came blundering in the front door like an unsuccessful retriever. 'Not in the Cottage, Miss Drew. What about upstairs?'

'It's all right, thanks, Monica,' replied Elizabeth. 'You can go back to your meal now. Tell Miss Dove I'll be in shortly.'

The medical student gave her a puzzled glance, but did as she was told. Elizabeth waited until the door of the dining-room closed after her, then she turned towards the bell-rope that the lay sisters rang to call the Warden or Mother Tobias to the parlour.

8

The Warden came floating along the passage in answer to the bell, still gently masticating her interrupted supper.

'Why, Elizabeth! Is anything the matter?'

The girl put a finger to her lips and nodded towards the dining-room door. They could hear one of the students chanting, 'porcupines, pineapples, plates, pewter—'

'What in the world?' began Mother Paul.

'Just a game. Reverend Mother, I think another student has disappeared. We can't locate Heather Markham.'

A shadow, like a cloud passing over a limpid serene pool, disfigured the nun's face. For a moment Elizabeth was allowed to see the pain in her eyes. 'Are you quite sure, Elizabeth?'

'She was not at supper. We sent someone over to the Cottage and I searched upstairs. Unless you or Mother Tobias gave her a late pass?'

The Warden turned and glided swiftly to the office. Elizabeth followed and found her opening the leave book which the girls always signed when they were given permission to stay out.

Mother Paul closed it with a snap. 'No, the child didn't have leave. When was she last seen?'

'I don't know. I didn't like to question the girls before telling you. The last time I saw her was here in the Hall when the rag was on. She was right behind me when you told me to open the front door. She wasn't in at tea-time. I was looking for her especially then. I was going to try getting her to talk about Maureen Mornane.'

The Warden gave her a swift, expressive glance, then sat down at the desk, resting her hands tensely on the edge.

'Mother Paul, this is frightful! You don't think that because of Maureen—?'

Elizabeth was swiftly interrupted. 'It is foolish and idle to speculate at this stage. We may even be unnecessarily alarmed.'

Elizabeth, who had been standing irresolutely on the threshold, turned her head as the dining-room door opened. Monica Carew came out, saw Elizabeth across the hall and seemed to hesitate.

'Yes, what is it, Monica?'

The medical student crossed the hall with her awkward, gangly stride. 'I was thinking about Heather, Miss Drew. She wasn't at the psychology lecture after lunch either.'

'Come into the office, Monica. Reverend Mother is here.'

'Oh, crumbs!' muttered the girl nervously. 'Why did I butt into it?'

The Warden looked over her shoulder. 'When did you last see Heather Markham?'

Monica edged into the room, shuffling her large feet. 'After lunch. Heather and I both had the same lecture to attend. We were just crossing the road from here when all of a sudden. Heather said not to wait for her as she wanted to make a phone call. She shot off to the public telephone booth down the road. But she didn't turn up to the lecture after all.'

'And that was the last you saw of her. How did she seem?'

'Okay, I think,' the girl replied vaguely. 'Perhaps not quite as chatty as usual. You know how you think of these things later—could be my imagination. But I do remember thinking at the time why she wanted to waste her money, when she could have made her call from here.' Monica was poor and cheeseparing notions were important.

'Odd!' agreed Mother Paul. 'Can you remember what Heather was wearing?'

'Some sort of floral thing, wasn't it?' Monica appealed to Elizabeth. 'The same as she wore at lunch, and her gown of course. Oh—and she was carrying that satchel she uses for her books and things.'

The Warden did some mysterious fumbling under her scapular, and produced a fountain pen and a notebook. 'About five feet five, plump build, straight brown hair, dressed in a cotton frock patterned in red, yellow and brown on a white background—'

Monica regarded her with awe. 'I say, fancy being able to remember all that detail.'

'—under a black college gown and beige-coloured—what do the young girls call those shoes, Elizabeth?'

'Flatties.'

'Yes, that is the word. Now, Monica, did any of the other girls see Heather later on?'

She shook her head. 'I must have been the last!' She paused and when Mother Paul did not speak, she asked, 'Is that all you want to ask?'

'Yes, you may go—and thank you for coming forward. I would appreciate it if you would refrain from talking too much about Heather until the position becomes clearer.'

'I'm not a gossip,' said Monica gruffly. 'But—but you don't really think anything could have happened to her, do you?'

Again the Warden was silent. Monica looked at Elizabeth who, with a movement of her head, indicated to the student to go.

Mother Paul consulted another page of her pocket book, lifted the telephone receiver and dialled a number. 'Come in and close the door, please, Elizabeth.'

The girl did as she was told and listened to what the Warden was saying.

'I wish to get in touch with Inspector Savage on a matter of great importance. This is the Warden of Brigid Moore Hall at the University speaking. Would you kindly ask him to come here at once, as we think another student has disappeared? Thank you!' She replaced the receiver and folded back the edge of her veil to look at Elizabeth. 'If Heather comes in safe and sound later. I'll be only too happy to look foolish.'

The girl smiled ruefully. 'And I will be only too happy to share your pillory.'

The nun beamed on her. 'I find your loyalty so comforting, dear—such a prop when one has so many doubts about one's judgement. Now I think our best move while we are waiting for the inspector is to employ the good Miss Dove's services. If she could assemble the girls in the recreation room and keep a tactful control over them, it would be such a help. We don't want them running all over the house becoming excited.'

Savage came to the door unaccompanied, but Elizabeth, delegated to the duty of admitting him, saw a police car in the driveway containing two other men besides the driver.

'In here, please, Inspector.' She indicated the parlour where the Warden was awaiting him.

Savage glanced automatically around the sparsely decorated room, then addressed the nun quietly. 'I received your message. Reverend Mother.'

'So kind of you to come so quickly. I hope I may be wrong, Inspector, but one of the students has been missing since early afternoon. Heather Markham.'

He frowned and glanced at Elizabeth. 'Markham?'

'Yes, the girl we think might know something of Maureen Mornane.'

'There is no possible explanation of where Miss Markham could be?'

'None,' replied the Warden. She told him about Monica Carew's information, and gave him the notes she had made regarding Heather's appearance.

'I'll just slip out to the car and have this sent to Headquarters. Our patrols will be circulated within seconds to keep an eye out for the girl.'

While he was gone Elizabeth said to the Warden, 'I think Heather must have come back here instead of going on to her lecture. That satchel Monica mentioned is in her room. She came back and started writing a letter home.'

'How odd!' remarked the nun. 'Surely that was not the whole reason for returning. Run upstairs and get it, will you, Elizabeth?'

Elizabeth sped off again, flipping down light switches as she went. But when she came to Heather's room there was no need to turn on the light. Judith Mornane had already done that. She was standing near the desk, calmly reading Heather's letter.

'What are you doing?' demanded Elizabeth sharply. 'No one is supposed to leave the recreation room.'

The girl flushed and tried childishly to hide the letter behind her.

'Give me that, Judith!'

She gave up the sheets. 'I wasn't doing anything wrong, truly, Miss Drew. I—I was only looking for clues so as to—to help.'

Elizabeth relaxed her severity. The police are more competent to do that, Judith. Go back downstairs and don't try to play detective again.'

'Did Mother Paul tell them about Maureen?' asked the girl eagerly. 'You know, if anything has—has happened to Heather, it will be on account of Maureen.'

Elizabeth pushed her gently out of the room, locked the door, and pocketed the key. 'Why do you say that?'

'Because Heather knew something. She told me she did—well, hinted, anyway. She came to my room after lunch. I'd been crying—the rag, you know. She told me not to be so upset—that perhaps the rag wasn't such a bad thing after all. She said something that sounded like Miss Dove—"an ill will—"' Judith stumbled over the proverb.

'It's an ill wind that blows nobody any good. What did Heather mean precisely?'

'She wouldn't say—except that she thought something was rather odd. I tried to persuade her, but all she would say in that prissy way of hers was that it wouldn't be right to say anything yet—that what she considered odd might only be a coincidence.'

They had reached the foot of the stairs. Savage, returning through the front door, saw the two girls and waited. Elizabeth led Judith up to him. 'This is Inspector Savage, Judith. Maureen Mornane's sister, Inspector.'

He took her hand kindly as she stared at him with wide, frightened eyes. 'So you're the young lady who insists murder was done. The search for your sister has never been given up, Judith.'

The girl's arm quivered under Elizabeth's hand. 'No, Maureen is dead!' she declared, in a suppressed voice. 'I know she is—and now it's Heather.'

'We'd better go back to the parlour,' suggested Elizabeth, with an apprehensive glance at the recreation room door.

Mother Paul was waiting for them. She smiled encouragingly at the student. 'Yes, I was going to send for you, Judith. Come in and sit down quietly, dear child.'

'Heather does know something about Maureen,' said Elizabeth. 'Tell Mother Paul and the inspector, Judith.'

They listened closely to the girl's faltering words. 'Something rather odd,' repeated the Warden softly. 'You are quite sure Heather gave you no further hint?'

Judith shook her head, then, with a timid glance at Elizabeth, added, 'She must have come back here after her lectures. Her satchel is in her room and there is a letter she was writing to her father. Miss Drew has it.'

'May I see it?' requested Savage.

Elizabeth passed it to him. 'Heather didn't attend any lectures this afternoon, Judith. She started off with Monica, then, for some reason, changed her mind. But before returning here she made a telephone call which I think I can account for. Margaret Knight, the housekeeper at Manning, told me this afternoon that Heather rang and wanted to speak to the Rector.'

Savage glanced up from Heather's letter. Elizabeth explained about the rag and Heather's officious complaints.

'She had no business taking matters into her own hands, but that is the sort of girl she is.'

'Unable to mind her own business, I take it,' said Savage. 'You can tell that from this letter. Would you read it aloud please, Mother Paul? Then if there is anything in it, that could give a clue to her whereabouts.'

The Warden put on her reading glasses and inspected the letter. 'It is addressed to her father. I remember her telling me her mother died some years ago. "*I have been neglecting you shamefully, but so much has been happening here that time just slips away. I hope you are wearing that vest I knitted for you during the vacation, and when the really cold weather starts—*"' The Warden broke off, running one finger down the page. 'Such a list of instructions for his welfare. I wonder if he will follow them all, poor man.'

Savage looked over her shoulder. 'Continue from here, where Heather mentions your name.'

Brows faintly raised, Mother Paul went on. ' "*We have a new Warden at Brigid Moore—a dear, but rather vague and helpless and not at all the sort of person to cope with the shocking things that have been happening here*" —'

'What a cheek!' muttered Judith indignantly.

—' "*I have been doing all I can to smooth matters out, but I don't think we will have complete peace until we find out what really happened to that girl who disappeared last year. You remember I told you about Maureen Mornane? Such a funny girl she was! You know how I always make it my business to help the freshettes settle in, but Maureen was quite impossible. I remember the first day she was here. I went into her room to have a friendly chat while she was unpacking.*"

When I asked her where she was from—"' Mother Paul came to the end of a page, and turned the sheets looking for more.

'No, that is all she wrote,' said Savage.

'Why did she stop so abruptly? Was she interrupted, do you think?'

'Perhaps. Where was this letter found?'

'On the floor of her room,' said Elizabeth. 'The curtains had brushed it off her desk.'

'Her desk is under a window? Which way does it face?'

'It looks out over Cemetery Road.'

They waited for the inspector to speak. After a pause he asked, 'What time did Heather and this other student, Monica, part?'

'Their lecture was at two, but they were probably running late because of the rag.'

'How long would it take them to get to the gates of the University?'

'Only a few minutes. Then Heather went down to the corner telephone booth.'

'That means that she was probably back here about two-thirty. Did no one see her return?'

'Everyone would have been gone by then,' said Elizabeth. 'Mother Tobias or one of the sisters may have seen her come back.'

'I'll inquire, Inspector,' suggested Mother Paul. 'But they would have been in their own part of the house which faces the back premises.'

Savage acknowledged this information with a brief nod. 'Then Heather went upstairs to her room, dropped her satchel and gown and began this letter. That could take her movements up to about three. Three o'clock,' he repeated thoughtfully. 'Where did she go then?'

Again the others watched him anxiously in silence. 'This Miss Knight at Manning College,' he said presently. 'I'd like to have a word with her. She may be able to fix the time of that telephone call more accurately.'

9

The police car was still in the driveway, but now only the driver was in it. He was reading a paper-backed thriller by the light of a torch, which he put hastily aside as they approached.

'Such a busman's choice of reading matter,' Mother Paul whispered to Elizabeth and Judith, while Savage inquired for news from Headquarters.

Savage carefully noted the time by his watch and requested them to lead the way Heather and Monica would have taken that afternoon. 'Nothing from Headquarters, by the way. My other two men are searching the University grounds.'

They arrived at the north gates and Elizabeth indicated the faint light from the telephone booth at the end of the road. The inspector left them, stepping out briskly. Presently he returned and again checked his watch. 'Now, which is the way to Manning College?'

Miss Knight opened the door to them. For a moment she regarded the group with surprise. 'May we come in, please, Margaret?' asked Elizabeth.

The housekeeper opened the door wider and they stepped into the tiled hall. 'I didn't know the Rector was expecting visitors. He's in his study. I'll go and tell him.'

'No, just a minute!' Elizabeth stopped her. 'Reverend Mother, this is Miss Knight, Inspector Savage from Russell Street, Margaret. And Miss Mornane, one of the students.'

'Pleased to meet you,' she returned grudgingly. She looked from one to the other uncertainly, and finally fastened on Judith. 'Mornane! You're the girl they're talking about, I suppose. Just like your sister to look at too.' She saw Judith stiffen and added quickly. 'Sorry! Her disappearing like that without a word must be ever so upsetting.'

The Warden said quietly. 'We've come here because another student has disappeared without a word—Heather Markham.'

Miss Knight stared at her. 'Not Miss Grand Manners! What's happened to her?'

'I understand Miss Markham spoke to you on the telephone this afternoon,' said Savage.

Margaret transferred her stare. 'Yes, that's right. How did you—? Oh, I suppose Miss Drew told you. She wanted to complain to the Rector about my boys' bit of fun at Brigid Moore but I wouldn't let her. Fancy—a bit of a kid like her! Did you ever know such a cheek, as I said to Miss Drew?'

'Miss Knight, can you recall as accurately as possible the time Miss Markham rang?'

'You do sound grim. Let me think now. It was some time after three because I'd just got in with the extra cakes for the party and it was just on to the hour when I was in the shop. Say about half-past when she rang, but I wouldn't like to swear to it. Now, what have I said wrong?'

'Nothing wrong, Miss Knight. It is known that Miss Markham intended making a call from the box in Cemetery Road about two. It was concluded that that call was to you.'

'No one rang here at two that I know of,' returned the house-keeper defensively. 'Certainly not Miss Nosey Parker.'

The inspector turned to Mother Paul. 'You have a telephone, of course?'

'The students have their own line in their recreation room.'

'Then it seems highly likely that Heather was still at the Hall at three-thirty. Miss Knight, you're quite sure Heather's remarks were confined wholly to complaining about the rag?'

'Of course I'm sure,' she returned sharply. 'Mind, I didn't listen too closely once I knew what she wanted. I just can't abide tattlers or moaners.'

'I see,' said Savage, deceptively smooth. 'You're sure but you weren't paying too much attention.'

Miss Knight gave him a suspicious glance, and said aggressively, 'Well, I did tell the Rector about her ringing, if you mean I didn't do the right thing. But I'd like to know how you expected me to think Miss Nosey's moans were all that important.'

'I would like to see the Rector now, please,' said Savage, cutting her hostility short.

'You'll find him in his study. Down the passage to the last door. Don't mind if I don't show you the way, but I've got other things to do.' With a muttered aside to Elizabeth, she left them.

They filed down the passage. Savage leading the way.

An incongruous cacophony of noise filtered up to meet them.

'Dear me!' remarked Mother Paul mildly. 'Are you sure that belligerent young woman gave us the right direction?'

Judith gave a nervous giggle. 'It sounds awfully like "Saint Louis Blues"!'

Savage knocked loudly. When the door was opened, Joe Daniels's beat hit them forcibly. Timothy put his long neck out, regarding them with surprise. 'Oh, hello! Elizabeth, what are you doing here? Father Hopkins!' He drew in his peck. 'Visitors for you.'

'Send them in, Tim!'

Timothy held the door wide, his smile directed on his fiancée. 'What is this? A deputation?' he whispered. 'Or have you come to join the jam session?'

She replied in an urgent undertone, 'Another of the girls has disappeared. We've called the police.'

'Your nice inspector?'

She nodded and turned her attention to the others.

The Rector had hastily put his pipe aside and switched off the record player. 'Caught at my two vices,' he announced cheerfully.

When Elizabeth made the introductions, he shook hands with Savage but spoke first to Mother Paul. 'I was going to call on you tomorrow. How does the new Warden find Brigid Moore Hall?'

'Somewhat disturbing. But I daresay dear Mother Provincial did not take murder into account when she appointed me.'

The Rector's sunken eyes widened. 'How remiss of her! I heard the rumour, but hardly liked to credit it.' He glanced at the others and Judith tried to hide behind Elizabeth.

Savage said in a tone of quiet authority, 'Please continue to regard it as a rumour even though Mother Paul has some grounds for her suspicions. Perhaps more so now that a second student has disappeared—which is why we are here. Your housekeeper spoke to this second girl on the telephone just prior to her vanishing.'

'Margaret? You wish to interview her, Inspector?' asked the Rector, clearing chairs of records and inviting them to sit down.

'I've already seen Miss Knight. It seems the student—Heather

Markham—tried to get in touch with you about the—er—rag some Manning students staged at Brigid Moore at lunch-time.'

'Oh, yes! Margaret mentioned something of the kind to me just before this afternoon's reception.'

He turned again to Mother Paul. 'By the way, I believe the chief culprit has already served some of his sentence in your garden. His alacrity in accepting his punishment quite amazed me. There'll be others over at the week-end, as I promised Miss Drew.'

'I wonder if he saw anything of Heather. Do you think Inspector Savage could talk to him for a few minutes?'

'Certainly. Tim, would you go up and ask young Baynes to come to my study? He has the room next to yours.'

'He's the one who is keen on Fiona,' whispered Judith to Elizabeth. 'She said he only came over to see her.'

They waited in silence until Timothy returned. He was followed by a young man wearing a tattered gown hastily thrown over a hulking yellow pullover and crumpled grey trousers.

The Rector introduced him. 'Inspector Savage wants to ask you a few questions, Peter.'

Elizabeth, watching the boy's face closely, thought she saw a guarded look in his eyes. 'What sort of questions?'

The Rector began to refill his pipe. 'It seems another Brigid Moore student has disappeared.'

'Oh? Which one?'

'Heather Markham,' supplied Mother Paul, who was also regarding him attentively.

'Heather? The fat girl with the mousey hair? I barely know her.'

'But I take it you do know her by sight at least,' said Savage. 'I understand you were gardening at Brigid Moore this afternoon, Mr Baynes. At what time?'

The boy inspected his ingrained hands, then thrust them into his pockets. 'Round about three. I can't say exactly.'

'Did you see anyone?'

'I saw the Sister in the kitchen. She told me where to find spades and things.'

'Did you see any of the students?'

'There was no one around,' he returned disinterestedly.

'What part of the garden were you working in?'

'The side,' said Baynes, adding bitterly, 'Where some fool—I mean, where some beastly prickly stuff is planted.'

'And you didn't see anyone come or go the whole time you were there?'

The student glanced around cautiously. 'I didn't see anyone—precisely. What I mean to say is—you want me to be strictly accurate, don't you? Well, I may have heard someone.'

'Oh? And what did you hear precisely?' asked Savage.

'Movements; I suppose you could call them that. A skulking sort of noise.'

'Where was the location of this noise?'

The boy thought for a moment. 'On the other side of the garden, where the lecture room is.'

'A separate building from the house, Inspector.' The Warden explained. 'It's known as the Cottage.'

Savage gave her a brief glance, then asked Baynes, 'Did you, by any chance, glance towards the house and see anyone at the upper windows?'

'I didn't see anyone except the kitchen Sister until the students came back for tea. I knocked off then as I'd just about had it anyway. I got back here about five.'

'Thank you, Mr Baynes.'

'That will be all then, Peter,' said the Rector pleasantly. 'You may go.'

The Warden got up suddenly. 'May I ask a question?' she requested, in her gentle voice.

Baynes took his hands out of his pockets and turned back, but avoided her eyes.

'You caused quite a deal of annoyance at lunch today,' she told him gravely. 'What made you and your friends think of such an exploit?'

He reddened and stammered. 'I don't know. It seemed a pretty good joke—at first. Topical, if you know what I mean.'

'Yes, I think I know what you mean. Was a similar rag held last year when Maureen's actual disappearance occurred? That would have been topical too, would it not? Or did you centre last year's rag around another incident of topical interest—the accidental drowning of Professor Craske's wife?'

Elizabeth caught her breath. She glanced at the inspector who was watching the two figures in the centre of the room closely. Then she saw the Rector regarding his student, a frown creasing his dome-like forehead.

Baynes was very pale. His hands twitched. He thrust them, clenched, back into his pockets. 'I don't remember what last year's rag was about,' he muttered. 'I wasn't in it.'

Savage caught the Warden's eye, a question in his glance. 'But you do remember Mrs Craske's death?' he asked the boy.

'I—I suppose so.'

'Did you know Mrs Craske—personally, I mean?'

Baynes moistened his lips. 'A—a little. A lot of undergrads knew her.'

'Then her death must have been a shock to a great many people,' suggested Savage smoothly.

'Oh, it was—it was!' the boy agreed eagerly.

Savage regarded him thoughtfully for a moment. 'Very well, you may go.'

'What was all that about?' Timothy whispered to Elizabeth, as the boy backed uncertainly out of the room.

'He was one of Helena Craske's protégés. Miss Dove must have told Mother Paul.'

'I don't like your being in this business, Elizabeth,' he said, in a worried voice. 'Is that inspector of yours seriously considering the possibility of foul play?'

'We think Heather knew something about Maureen Mornane's disappearance,' she replied quietly, as she got up in answer to a signal from the Warden. 'Tim, it's my college. I can't help being concerned.'

The Rector was speaking to Savage. 'Quite a disturbing business, as Reverend Mother truly remarked. We can't have our students being spirited away like this. If there is anything I can do—?' He turned his head as Miss Knight suddenly slipped into the room.

'A man on the phone, speaking from Brigid Moore,' she announced brusquely. 'He wants the inspector to come back at once. He says they've found the missing Markham girl.'

10

'Time is a great healer,' declared Miss Dove bravely, 'but I assure you. Reverend Mother, it is going to take me a long time to get over the terrible shock I received.'

It was going on for midnight and the three women—the Warden, Elizabeth and the Science tutor—were in the Cottage sitting-room. Occasional ominous sounds and strange curt remarks wafted in from the lecture room.

There had been a definite wobble in Miss Dove's last words, and the Warden said comfortingly. 'Yes, I'm sure it will, Miss Dove. But your calmness has been wonderful. How relieved I am that it was you who found the poor child, and not one of the students.'

'They would have gone to pieces at once,' agreed Miss Dove, squaring her shoulders in tribute to the compliment. But she added to Elizabeth, 'To think that you and I might have spent the night here in the Cottage little realizing that only a few yards away was poor Heather—dead!'

Elizabeth said nothing. She was feeling confused and immeasurably weary, and her colleague had said something similar only a few minutes before. She marvelled at Mother Paul's patience as Miss Dove recounted once more her discovery of Heather Markham's body.

'I had just sent the girls off to bed. Reverend Mother—and quite a job it was too. They all wanted to go out looking for Heather. Too many cooks spoil the broth, I told them. Then I made the rounds with Mother Tobias and, after locking up, came across to the Cottage. Of course, had I but known what I was to discover here'—she gave a shudder—'I would never have ventured forth, for all there was a policeman in our drive. Never will I forget the sight when I opened the locker in the lecture room. That poor girl with her face all purple and swollen, hanging by her own belt!'

Elizabeth welcomed with relief the appearance at the sitting-room door of Inspector Savage.

But Miss Dove would not stop. 'I was just telling them, Inspector, that the body could have been there all night if I hadn't happened to be looking for my gown. Everyone uses that locker to hang things in, you know.'

Elizabeth's eyes caught Mother Paul's and she quelled the awful giggle that welled up involuntarily.

But Inspector Savage apparently did not see any macabre humour in what Miss Dove had said. 'My men have finished their work now, and an ambulance has taken the body away. My advice is to go to bed, and try and forget what has happened.' He glanced at the Warden. 'Perhaps if you have some strong sedative in the house?'

She nodded. 'I'll see to it. You are leaving now, Inspector?'

'I want to get down to the morgue. But I'll be back first thing in the morning.'

'I'll come and see you off.'

Left alone with Elizabeth, Miss Dove expostulated, 'Some things are easier said than done. I know I won't sleep a wink even with a sedative. As for forgetting what has happened—! I'll never be able to erase the memory of that bloated face, with the tongue—'

'Be quiet!' interrupted Elizabeth harshly. 'Talking about Heather won't help you to forget.'

Miss Dove blinked in outraged astonishment. 'Well! I never imagined to hear you talk to me like that.'

Elizabeth got up and walked over to the fireplace. She didn't care if she had offended Miss Dove. At least it was the means of keeping her quiet. A stony silence was maintained for the prolonged time until the Warden returned. She seemed to sense the strained relations.

'Now, Miss Dove, I think you should take that nice sensible man's advice and go to bed. Here are two tablets which Mother Tobias assures me are highly efficient.'

But Miss Dove refused to be mollified. 'I can tell when I'm not wanted,' she announced huffily. She took the tablets and said good night with crushing formality.

The Warden closed the door, sighed and said absently. 'Just as well if she is a bit cross—such a nice ordinary emotion.'

Elizabeth smiled wearily. 'Are you suggesting that you and I should start getting on each other's nerves to the same purpose?'

'Don't be foolish, dear. You and I do not have to pretend.'

Elizabeth sat up. 'You mean you did want to get rid of Miss Dove?'

'Was I too obvious?' asked the Warden anxiously. 'So strange of her—looking for her gown in the cupboard when all the time it was in her room. I saw it there myself.'

Elizabeth looked at her. 'What are you trying to say?'

'That whatever else Miss Dove was looking for, it was certainly not her gown.'

Elizabeth hesitated, then said carefully, 'I know it seems fantastic Heather committing suicide, but what about that note Inspector Savage found in her pocket? You saw what she wrote.'

The nun drew out her notebook and reading glasses. 'I made a copy. Such a good notion to write things down, I find. Listen closely and tell me if I have Heather's words correctly. *I know what happened to Maureen Mornane. It is only a matter of time before I am questioned concerning her disappearance. I cannot go on.*' She looked up over her spectacles inquiringly.

'Yes, that is correct,' said the girl impatiently. 'Her intention is obvious. And the writing was Heather's. We all verified that when the inspector passed the note around. How can you suggest Miss Dove—?'

'I only suggest that it was strange of Miss Dove to say she was looking for her gown,' interrupted the Warden swiftly. 'Yes, it was Heather's note—a seeming suicide note—but don't you consider this point a bit odd? She knew what had happened to Maureen, but she did not reveal what. Surely before taking such a terrible step as committing suicide, she would have done so?'

'She must have been upset—deranged.'

'There was no hint of derangement about the letter she started to her father only a short time previously—no hint of what she was going to do.'

There was a pause. Then Elizabeth said helplessly, 'I don't understand.'

'No, neither do I,' replied the nun, with simple candour. She gazed at the girl thoughtfully for a moment, then slowly and deliberately she asked, 'But is it possible for anyone to hang herself on a hook in a cupboard, yet with her feet a good ten inches from the floor?'

'No—impossible!' Savage told Mother Paul some hours later in her office. 'Either the tips of her feet should have been touching the floor of the cupboard, or else we should have found some box or stool which she stood on and then kicked away.'

The Warden said quietly. 'Then it was murder.'

Savage nodded. 'Yes, Heather Markham must have been murdered. According to the post-mortem she died between three-fifteen and three forty-five from asphyxiation caused by strangulation with a narrow strap.'

Mother Paul glanced at him sharply. 'A narrow strap? But Heather's belt was one of those wide leather ones all the girls seem to wear at present.'

The inspector's tired face lightened in appreciation. 'I thought you'd spot that one, Mother Paul. Yes, Heather was strangled first and then hung up by her own belt in a not very good attempt to simulate suicide.'

'One should never commit murder in a hurry,' remarked the nun thoughtfully.

Savage hid a smile at this naïve observation. Then he said seriously. 'Perhaps it would be a good idea to let the suicide verdict stand for a while.'

'An excellent notion,' she agreed. 'You may rely upon my discretion.'

Savage frowned. 'The mystifying part of Heather's death is the suicide note. Our handwriting experts say it was quite definitely her writing, but it seems highly unlikely that she could have been coerced into writing such a letter.' He paused, eyeing the Warden quizzically. 'I don't suppose you have any suggestions in this matter.'

'Dictation,' replied Mother Paul promptly. 'Not Heather's confession—the murderer's. Such a managing conscientious girl—poor Heather. So easy for anyone with a little astuteness and guile to play on her weakness.'

'You mean the murderer suggested Heather write out the confession?' asked Savage incredulously.

The nun nodded. 'Why not? Don't you policemen take dictated statements, then get the person you're questioning to sign them? Heather probably only needed a little prompting to do the same. I daresay she was quite occupied with the task when she was strangled. Not that she knew she had her back turned to a murderer.

'All Heather realized was that this person simply knew something about Maureen Mornane's disappearance, and she wanted it in writing, so as to have definite proof.'

'That's a plausible theory,' conceded Savage. 'It means that the person standing behind Heather ready to strangle her as she wrote was someone about whom she had no fears.'

'Heather had no fears because she had not yet realized that two murders had been committed,' corrected the nun gently. 'She had to be silenced before she came to that realization.'

'Then whatever aroused Heather's suspicions was something small enough to be overlooked by most people.'

'Yes, that is so,' agreed the Warden. 'I can't help thinking it had something to do with that ridiculous rag.'

'The rag? You mean young Baynes from Manning College?'

The nun bent her head, saying unhappily. 'Please don't ask me anything more. It would never do to suggest someone guilty, without being quite, quite sure. So uncharitable!' Savage maintained his gravity with an effort. He blamed lack of sleep for his mixed emotions of exasperation and amusement.

'Neither would it be right of me to withhold information,' went on Mother Paul earnestly. 'I promise you most faithfully not to do that. I admit I have an idea what could have happened to Maureen Mornane, but I feel sure you would dismiss it out of hand at the moment.'

'You consider Maureen is the crux of this case and that her disappearance is due to the theory you put forward yesterday—that she was a witness to murder?'

Mother Paul stirred uncomfortably. 'Yes and no.'

Savage laughed shortly. 'I feel sure, Mother Paul, that your charity would not allow you to be deliberately tantalizing.'

She became distressed. 'Indeed no, Inspector. I am truly sorry, but I cannot reply with precision yet.'

'All right, all right,' he answered, trying not to sound testy. 'Let me put the matter another way. Was your assertion that Helena Craske—Professor Craske's wife—might have been murdered made seriously or merely as a suggestion?'

The nun fingered her rosary beads, passing them through her fingers restlessly. Then she lifted her head and said softly. 'Yes, Helena Craske must have been murdered.'

Savage gave her a close, silent scrutiny. He still could not decide whether he should be paying so much heed to a nun.

He gathered up his papers and rose. 'I am going to start this investigation from the beginning,' he announced curtly. 'Helena Craske, Maureen Mornane and Heather Markham. Three murders, but in that order.'

The Warden rose too. 'An excellent method of procedure,' she said warmly. 'I knew you would come to that decision sooner or later. I need have no further anxiety.'

Savage left her without speaking. He felt in rather a dazed condition—as though in the nicest possible way he had been told his own business.

II

A slightly different state of bemusement had settled upon the students of Brigid Moore Hall following the news of Heather Markham's alleged suicide. At first they had been inclined to discuss it—going round and round in circles to find some final explanation to the tragedy. But it remained as frighteningly incomprehensible to them as it had at first to Elizabeth. She listened to their subdued talk at breakfast, alert for signs of trouble or hysteria.

'But why did she do it?' asked Nola, thumping her closed hand on the table. 'Just tell me that—why?'

'The Warden said she was upset about the rag. She knew something about Maureen—something terrible.'

'I don't think we've been told the whole story,' another girl suggested angrily. 'I think we're being kept in the dark.'

'It isn't fair. We've a right to know.'

Monica Carew raised her eyes from the textbook she had propped against a sugar bowl. 'Pipe down!' she ordered curtly. 'Maybe it's better if we don't know.'

Silence fell after a few further mutters. They all had respect for Monica. Elizabeth returned her attention to her breakfast. She cast a sidelong glance at her colleague. Miss Dove's smooth face looked unusually worn and there were dark streaks under her eyes.

The mutters began again. 'The inspector who came last night is with the Warden now. I'd like to know what they are talking about.'

'We were all nice to Heather, weren't we?' appealed someone nervously. 'It can't have been anything we did that caused her to—to—'

'Be quiet! Of course we were nice. What a silly thing to say!'

'Well, there's no need to be rude. At least I'm being honest when I say none of us cared much for Heather. Perhaps she suddenly realized and—'

'You're talking rot, so dry up!'

Nola intervened, 'No scrapping! That won't get us anywhere either. What a ghastly business this is—we're all on edge.'

'If it were round about exam time I'd understand,' declared a student, trying to make a poor joke. 'We all feel suicidal then. But to happen at the beginning of term!'

'Too much has been happening since term began,' growled another, shooting a fulminating glance down the table towards Judith.

Fiona, who had been scowling silently at her all through the meal and taking no part in the discussion, suddenly shoved her plate away and got up. 'I suppose we'll come out of it in time,' she said, a touch of violence in her voice, 'but right now I don't want to talk or hear another word about Heather.' She flung out of the room, slamming the door behind her.

Miss Dove took a deep breath, as though wearily bracing herself to do her duty. 'Now, girls! It doesn't do to give way. We must keep our end up.' And she bravely ate a rissole to set a good example.

Judith caught Elizabeth's attention as the dining-room gradually cleared. 'Heather was murdered, wasn't she?' she whispered. 'I promise I won't say anything—you can trust me.' And she darted away before Elizabeth could expostulate.

Is it possible to trust anyone? thought Elizabeth bitterly, as she made her way out of the house. Fear, foreboding and violent death were scarcely breeding grounds for trust.

It was a clear, crisp morning with a hint of midday warmth to come. Elizabeth paused to slip into the cardigan she had previously been wearing across the shoulders of her blue-and-white spotted dress.

The leaves of the oak trees lining the driveway were starting to fall. Soon they would be choking up the gutters, and then with the first autumn rains the drive would become a morass. She made a mental note to suggest to the Warden that the Manning undergraduates should begin burning off. Then she thought of Peter Baynes and the sounds he had heard of someone in the grounds . . .

She was still standing in the driveway when Inspector Savage came out of the house and caught up with her. 'Good morning, Miss Drew,' he said quietly.

She started. 'Oh—good morning! You've been to see Mother Paul?'

He nodded ruefully. 'What is there about nuns that makes you do what they want, long before you actually realize that it is a good idea?'

Elizabeth laughed nervously. 'What has Mother Paul made you do now?'

'Go back to the beginning of this case—to the possible murder of Helena Craske.'

The girl moistened her lips. 'Helena?'

He glanced over his shoulder then back at Elizabeth. 'What is it you are trying not to look at, Miss Drew?' he asked whimsically.

'Nothing—at least—!'

A group of students hurried down the driveway, gowns flying from their bright cotton frocks. They cast scared eyes at their Humanities tutor's large, formidable companion and disappeared.

Elizabeth said quickly. 'I was thinking of Peter Baynes and what he said about the—the skulking noise of yesterday. Listen to our gate as the girls go out.' A heavy creak and clang sounded pat on cue.

'What are you suggesting, Miss Drew?'

She indicated the low fence behind him, just visible through the heavy shrubs. 'Supposing the noise was made by—by a person who did not wish to be seen. Instead of coming up the driveway it would be safer to enter the garden next door and climb the fence.'

He turned and surveyed the shrubbery. 'You might have something there, Miss Drew.' He moved along the narrow path which led to the Cottage, looking for a break in the foliage. Presently he entered at the spot where Elizabeth had halted the previous day when Craske had called to her.

He came out, brushing his clothes. 'It looks as though you are right, Miss Drew. That is Professor Craske's place, is it not? I was wanting an excuse to call on him too. I would like you to come with me if possible. Or have you other duties?'

'I can spare a few minutes,' she agreed reluctantly.

They moved down the driveway, the inspector saying, 'Your coming with me should make the visit more of a routine affair. I don't want to arouse undue suspicions, as I was telling Mother Paul. While we are working more or less in the dark, it will be better for all suspects to stay in the dark too.'

'I see what you mean,' replied Elizabeth, without enthusiasm.

They went into the place next door and up the shallow stone steps to the porch. Savage stood aside as Elizabeth rang the bell. When Craske opened the door he did not, at first, see her companion.

'Elizabeth! What a charming surprise! But must it be at such a mundane hour? I'm still having breakfast.'

The girl said stiffly, 'Professor Craske, this is Inspector Savage, from Russell Street.'

Craske opened the door wider so that the full splendour of his Paisley-patterned dressing-gown was visible. 'Indeed? Then you've come adequately protected, have you, Elizabeth? How do you do, Inspector. I can't say I'm delighted to know you, merely surprised.'

'May we come in. Professor? There are one or two questions I'd like to ask.'

Craske's brows went up. 'Certainly. I'm intrigued as to what they may be. I've read about policemen wanting to ask one or two questions. Why not three or four, I wonder? In here!'

He took them into a living-room which was not only untidy, but decidedly in need of cleaning. Elizabeth remembered it as a flowery scented background to the pale, languid woman who had been his wife. The only trace left of Helena was the long, low couch on which she had invariably reclined with a carefully careless draping of filmy negligées. Now it was covered with a conglomeration of books, papers and articles of masculine clothing that the owner of the house had dropped there heedlessly. There was a pair of shoes, a pullover or two, a collar still threaded with a tie and a plastic raincoat.

Craske sat down at a small table set in a sun-filled bay window. 'You don't mind if I go on eating, do you? Find somewhere to sit if you wish. You can easily observe this room lacks the feminine touch, Inspector. I like it that way, though it is a sore temptation to the ladies of my acquaintance.'

'I'll come straight to the point. Professor. Last night one of the students at the college next door was found dead. She had apparently hanged herself in a locker in the building known as the Cottage.'

Craske looked at Elizabeth, the nonchalant expression wiped from his face. 'How ghastly! Who was it?'

'A Social Studies student. Heather Markham.'

'I wouldn't have had any dealings with her,' he said quickly. 'That doesn't come under my Faculty.'

'I'm not suggesting you had, Professor,' replied Savage smoothly. 'But living next door to Brigid Moore Hall, I was wondering if you could help me in any way. For example, Miss Markham was reported missing after lunch yesterday, having been last seen going to the public telephone booth at the end of the road. Instead of attending the lecture at 2 p.m. as she should, she returned to her college. That means she must have passed this house.'

Craske snapped his fingers. 'Now you come to mention it, I did see a student coming up the road as I was leaving here. A short, plump lass.'

'What time was that?'

'Oh, about two-thirty, I suppose. I remember registering vaguely that she should be elsewhere at that time—lecture or study. Brigid Moore tutors must be getting lax—tut, Elizabeth!'

Savage intervened before the girl could retort. 'Miss Markham had just made a mysterious telephone call, the upshot of which was her return to Brigid Moore. Certain impressions suggest that she returned in order to see someone. Whether that person was a member of the household is not yet known, but someone did come surreptitiously to Brigid Moore about an hour later.'

Craske pushed his chair back and rose. 'Indeed? You sound very ominous, Inspector. I wonder if at this stage I should state that I did not return here until after five. I went straight from my classes to Manning College where a reception was being held.'

'You have saved me some devious questions, Professor,' rejoined Savage dryly. 'Tell me—have you ever observed anyone using your garden as a short cut to the building next door called the Cottage?'

The other paused in taking off his dressing-gown. 'No, I can't say I have.' He threw the dressing-gown to join the raincoat on Helena's couch and shrugged himself into a tweed jacket.

'I'm sorry I can't help you at all, Inspector. To be candid, I can't quite understand why you should have expected me to be able. You said this unfortunate girl committed suicide. Have you not discovered a reason for her so doing?'

'She left a note,' said Savage quietly. 'It seems she was afraid of being questioned in connexion with the disappearance of another student—Maureen Mornane.'

'Oh, I see. Then you are not so much interested in suicide as to what caused the suicide. Is that about it?'

'That's about it,' replied Savage. 'It has come to my knowledge. Professor, that this first girl, Maureen, was last seen apparently leaving this house on the morning your wife—died.'

Craske shot a quick glance at Elizabeth, who was sitting tensed and silent. 'Oh, it has, has it?' he said softly. 'I'm glad you said apparently, Inspector.'

'Did you or your late wife know this girl Mornane?'

'Helena may have. She had a habit of making fleeting friends among the undergraduates. She was something of an invalid and liked having young people dropping in to see her. The front door was never locked.'

'Then it is not out of the question that Maureen Mornane could have been calling here,' said the inspector, a hard note in his voice.

But Craske maintained his antagonizing nonchalance. 'I never saw the girl here, nor did I ever hear Helena talking about her as she usually did about the other youngsters.'

Savage pressed on ruthlessly. 'Then you must have known Maureen by sight—if you are able to state with such conviction that she had never visited here.'

Craske moved across to the couch and began to gather books and papers together. Presently he said provokingly. 'They tell me she had red hair. I can recall two or three redheads in my lecture theatre, but never in my house.'

'Very well. Professor,' said Savage, without signs of chagrin. 'Just one last question, were relations between you and your wife all that they should have been?'

There was a glint of anger in Craske's eyes. 'I refuse to answer that question,' he replied haughtily. 'Will you see Inspector Savage out, Elizabeth? I feel you owe me something for having brought him in.'

The girl got up, casting an uncertain glance at Savage. 'I'm sorry.' she said quietly.

The anger went out of his eyes, and he came to stand in front of her. 'I daresay you couldn't help it,' he replied carelessly, touching her cheek lightly with a forefinger. He glanced at his watch. 'I'm late for my first lecture, anyway. Good-bye, Inspector! I trust we will not meet again.'

After he had gone, Elizabeth turned away uncomfortably from Savage's thoughtful gaze. 'Well, we can't stand about in another man's house,' he said at last, and guided Elizabeth to the front door. 'Forgive the personal question, Miss Drew, but is Craske a close friend of yours?'

'Professor Craske invariably gives the impression that he is close friends with every female he knows,' she answered coldly.

To her surprise. Savage smiled. 'I feel properly snubbed, Miss Drew.'

12

As Savage and Elizabeth emerged from Craske's house, a young woman was coming up the garden path. Elizabeth recognized her as one of the maids from Manning College, and said, 'Good morning. Professor Craske has just left.'

'Just as well,' returned the young woman cheerfully. 'Miss Knight said I was to clean the living-room whether he likes it or not. Will he be mad!'

Elizabeth stepped off the porch, but Inspector Savage said, 'Just one moment! What is your name, please?'

'Thelma Young, if you really want to be nosey,' said the girl, with an inquiring glance at Elizabeth.

'How long have you been doing this particular job?'

'Well actually, I'm full time at Manning, but we help out occasion-ally—just to oblige, you might say. Miss Knight never minds, and it means a few extra bob.'

Thelma, wasn't it you or Mildred who found Mrs Craske in the bath?' asked Elizabeth suddenly.

'Yours truly, I'm sorry to say. Don't wake up that awful business, if you don't mind.'

But her tone and dramatic shudder indicated that she was only too ready to talk about it. 'Have you ever been questioned by the police?' Thelma demanded of Savage, who had been casting Elizabeth a glance of appreciation.

'No, I can't say I have,' he replied equably.

'Lucky you, then! It's something frightful? Nag, nag, nag—the same old questions over and over. How did I find her, what time was it, what was I doing here anyway—until I nearly had the hysterics.'

'You seem to have had a tough time,' said Savage sympathetically.

'You're telling me! You'd think they'd have had more considera-tion. As if finding her wasn't bad enough, and poor Professor Craske all white and shaking like a leaf. And the way they went on at him. He's such a nice gentleman, ever so friendly too. Why was she allowed to have a bath when no one was in the house? They reckoned she was an invalid, you see. But I've got my own opinion about that.'

'About what?' Savage coaxed her.

'About Mrs Craske being sick, chronic like. I reckon she was just after attention all the time. "Oh, Thelma!" she'd say, almost before I had my nose in the door. "Don't make so much clatter, I hardly slept a wink last night." And she'd moan on about her head or her back or what have you, and waste my time asking me to get her pink pills or her blue drops or some other fancy medicine. Another few days of my fine lady and I would have been screaming. So what that poor hubby of hers went through I wouldn't like to say.'

'Another few days?' repeated Savage. 'Then you weren't coming here very long before she died?'

Thelma regarded him with a momentary suspicion, but a second glance at Elizabeth seemed to reassure her.

'That was a real dirty trick Mildred played on me. "You go, Thel," she said, when Miss Knight was called away to the country to her aunty's funeral. "Ever so nice she is and got the loveliest negligées. It'll be a change for you after all the dirty shirts here."'

' "I don't mind which one of you goes," says Miss Knight. She gets a bit grand at times, but she's not a bad stick. But go someone must. I can't be in two places at once." But it struck me she was fed up with waiting on Madam herself and thought it was a good excuse to get from under, as the saying goes. But did she blow her top when she came back and heard about Madam? "You shouldn't have allowed her to take a bath all alone, Thelma," she says, just like the cops.'

'And what did you say?' asked Savage encouragingly.

'I said—' the girl giggled. '"Miss Knight, I can't be in two places at once, and even if the Rector does send me on useless messages, I am first and foremost employed by Manning College."'

'You were delayed in coming here on the morning Mrs Craske died—is that right? What was the useless message?'

'There was a parcel the Rector wanted picked up at the registrar's office,' explained Thelma, a note of grievance in her voice. 'So I trek all the way over to get it, but nobody knows what's which when I ask for it. Talk about messing around—I must have been there for a least half an hour.'

Savage shot a quick glance at Elizabeth, as though to acknowledge his appreciation once more. 'The registrar's office couldn't find the Rector's parcel? What did he say about that?'

'Nothing. That was the funny part. He didn't know anything about a parcel either.'

'But didn't you say the Rector—?'

Thelma broke in impatiently, 'You don't seem to get it. The Rector didn't tell me to go to the registrar's office. Someone rang up and said, "Is that you, Thelma?" so I says, "Yes, what can I do for you?" Then the voice says, "There's a parcel at the registrar's office that has to be delivered to the Rector double quick." So I says, "Okay, I'll come over and get it." And there we are! Funny business when you come to think of it, wasn't it? What I mean is—if it hadn't been for that wild goose chase, I might have stopped Madam from drowning in her bath.'

Savage said quickly, 'Well, it's all over now, Thelma, and talking won't bring Mrs Craske back. Just one point, however—was it a man or woman who made that call? Now think carefully.'

'I would have said it was a woman,' she replied uncertainly. 'There are only girls at the office, anyway, aren't there, Miss Drew?'

'Is there a chance that it might have been the voice of a man trying to sound like a woman?' asked Savage.

Thelma looked at him vacantly. 'Why should anyone want to do that? I'm sure I don't know what you're getting at.' She turned to Elizabeth. 'I haven't said anything wrong, have I?'

'No, nothing wrong, Thelma. And we mustn't keep you from your work any longer.'

Savage took the hint and stepped off the porch. Thelma called after him, 'If you're a friend of the Professor's, don't let on that I've been gossiping about his affairs, will you? He's always treated me so nice.'

He gave her a reassuring smile and wave. 'I won't say anything.'

In the street beyond the cypress hedge. Savage said to Elizabeth, Thank you, Miss Drew. You must have been inspired. Strange how the printed word can differ in interpretation from the spoken word. In the inquest report on Mrs Craske the fact that the daily help was late on the morning of her death sounds far less important than what we heard direct from Thelma.'

'You think she was deliberately delayed?' asked Elizabeth anxiously.

'I'd like to hear Father Hopkins's version of this urgent parcel at the registrar's office first.'

'You realize that your questioning of Thelma regarding the Craskes will be all over the University—plus embellishments,' said Elizabeth resentfully.

He shrugged. 'Unfortunate, but it can't be helped.'

'It seems hardly fair on Professor Craske. It could mean his resignation if there is any suspicion that his wife was—was—' she floundered as she met his stern gaze.

'Murder concerns foul, not fair, play, Miss Drew.'

'Yes, of course,' she agreed unhappily.

Presently he said, more sympathetically, 'Murder investigation is always a distasteful business. Tell me, who lives on this side of the Craske house?'

'The Whipples. He is one of the Deans.'

'Was that Mrs Whipple watering the garden while we were talking to Thelma?'

Elizabeth looked up startled. 'I didn't notice Mrs Whipple.'

'I don't think we were supposed to notice her,' replied Savage dryly. 'Suppose we stroll past and you can satisfy the lady's curiosity as to who I am.'

Hose in hand, Mrs Whipple had taken up a strategic point near the front fence. She was wearing a brunch coat patterned with startling bunches of flowers, grubby bedroom slippers, and her dyed hair was wrapped in a turban of pink net. 'Hey there!' she called jocularly, eyeing Savage in an unabashed fashion. 'What's happened to Tiny Tim, Miss Drew? You two had a row?'

'Mrs Whipple, this is Inspector Savage, from Russell Street.'

Mrs Whipple looked him up and down again. 'My, you are a big fellow! I like a man with a bit of brawn on his bones. That Doctor Timothy of Miss Drew's had better fatten himself up if he doesn't want to be cut out.'

Elizabeth said loudly. 'Inspector Savage is here in an official capacity, Mrs Whipple. A shocking thing happened last night. One of our girls committed suicide.'

'So Eddie and I heard—hanged herself, poor kid! Do you know why she did it, Inspector? Or shouldn't I be asking?'

'No, it is quite in order to ask. From the note that we found, it seems the girl was concerned about possible questioning in regard to the disappearance of a student called Maureen Mornane.'

'Oh, that business! Rumours have been flying these past few days. I believe the sister is making all sorts of wild accusations. Perhaps she'll learn to mind her tongue now that she's seen the effect of her words on the poor Markham kid.'

Savage rested his hands on the brick fence. 'How did you know it was the Markham girl, Mrs Whipple?' he asked smoothly.

Her eyes narrowed and she shook a finger at him, laughing. 'Oh, you policemen! Always trying to catch people out. Gwen Dove came rushing over to tell us first thing this morning. She wept all over Eddie's clean shirt. Eddie's my old man, as I suppose you've gathered by now. You must meet him some time.'

'I'd like to,' said Savage. 'Tell me, Mrs Whipple, did Miss Dove mention the note that Heather Markham left?'

She eyed him warily. 'Maybe she did. What about it?'

'I was wondering why you should have asked me for a reason for Heather's suicide. Miss Dove must have told you.'

'I asked because I reckon there's more in your being around than meets the eye,' she told him bluntly. 'And I've just got as much right to know what's going on as Miss Drew here.'

'All right,' said Savage agreeably. 'What do you want to know?'

She hunched a plump shoulder. 'Now you're trying to soft-soap me. All I want to know is why you're inquiring into Heather Markham's death when she committed suicide?'

'That seems a fair demand. But I did not say I was inquiring into the girl's death, Mrs Whipple. My interest lies in what Heather knew of Maureen Mornane's whereabouts.'

Mrs Whipple moved along the fence to direct the hose's spray on some late-blooming phlox. 'You're not regarding the sister's nonsense seriously, are you? I thought you people said that Maureen Mornane must have done a bunk because she wanted to.'

Elizabeth, trailing reluctantly after Savage, heard him repeat what he had said to Mother Paul at their first meeting. 'Whether Maureen disappeared willingly or unwillingly, her case has never been regarded as closed, Mrs Whipple.'

Her voice rose stridently. 'Really, Inspector, are you allowing an hysterical country schoolgirl to make a fool of you?'

'I'd rather be made a fool of than be fooled, Mrs Whipple.'

She shrugged. 'All right! Don't say I didn't warn you. I daresay you think you're only doing your duty. What do you intend to do now, Inspector? Start digging up the University grounds in search of the Mornane girl's body?'

He gazed about her well-kept garden speculatively. 'We'll delay that laborious task until we can restrict the area.'

Mrs Whipple said quickly, 'The Dean and I were away at the time of the disappearance. You remember that, don't you, Miss Drew? We came back just in time for Helena Craske's funeral. The police were inquiring about Maureen then.'

'Yes, that is so,' agreed Elizabeth, embarrassed by the appeal. Stripped of her vigour and vulgarity, Mrs Whipple seemed a pathetic figure. To hide her discomfiture, Elizabeth glanced at her watch, saying, 'I really must be going.'

'I'll come with you,' said Savage. 'Then you cannot offer any further suggestions about Maureen, Mrs Whipple?'

'What do you mean—further suggestions?' she demanded suspiciously. 'I know nothing about the girl.'

'I mean other than to start digging,' he replied gravely.

'Oh, go on with you!' she said good-humouredly, but Elizabeth saw her hand tremble and then grip the fence.

They walked on and Savage said quietly, 'As the Whipples were away at the times of Mrs Craske's death and Maureen's disappearance no suspicion can be attached to them. That being so, why is Mrs Whipple showing signs of apprehension, Miss Drew?'

Elizabeth was silent for a moment. Then she said in a suppressed voice, 'Oh, this is hateful! Some people don't care much for Mrs Whipple, but the Dean is very much liked and admired. And she is devoted to him.'

'You are suggesting she is nervous for her husband's sake? Did he know Maureen?'

'He couldn't have known her. You heard what she said about their being away. They have a holiday cottage down the Bay somewhere. The reason why they weren't back at the beginning of term was that she was ill.'

'But there is something that you are not happy about, Miss Drew. Tell me, please.'

Elizabeth gripped her books hard. 'I can only tell you what I know by hearsay—and that is not reliable evidence, is it? It concerns Helena Craske. She and the Whipples were very friendly at one time. Then quite suddenly Mrs Whipple broke off the friendship. The Dean continued to call at the Craskes' place, but—but not always when Professor Craske was there.'

'I see,' said Savage slowly.

'The Whipples seem quite friendly with Professor Craske now. They were wonderful to him when Helena died.'

'This Bayside place they have—wouldn't it be within commuting distance of the University?'

Elizabeth opened her mouth to reply, then stopped. Her eyes grew more troubled. 'Yes, Professor Whipple must have come up,' she said at last. 'I remember now. Miss Dove said when she broke the news of Helena's death to Professor Craske, he was with the Dean.'

'I see,' said Savage again. 'Well, I can't follow that lead up until I come out into the open about Mrs Craske. You have been very patient and of invaluable assistance, Miss Drew. I'm sorry to have claimed so much of your time.'

'That's all right,' the girl replied awkwardly. 'What are you intending to do now?'

'Call on the Rector of Manning College. I want to try and establish that Thelma the maid was deliberately hoaxed into being late at the Craske house. I'd like you to come with me if you would. I want you to report what has been going on to your Warden.'

'Mother Paul? She will appreciate the courtesy.'

'No courtesy,' replied Savage ruefully. 'That remarkably shrewd nun of yours knows more than she will admit at present. If I can, as it were, feed her with outside information she might happen on some clue that will lead her into confiding frankly in me. At the moment I respect her reticence. From experience most people are only too willing to pour out wild theories and suppositions.'

Elizabeth wondered if his words contained an admonition, and hastily cast her mind over what she herself had said.

Savage smiled, as though reading her thoughts. 'And she couldn't have chosen a more prudent liaison officer.'

The door of Manning College stood open and a group of undergraduates came out as Elizabeth and Savage approached. They glanced in furtive recognition at the tutor and then curiously at the inspector.

Miss Knight came bustling down the back passage, a bowl of freshly arranged flowers held out in front of her. She had evidently been picking over the remnants of the previous day's floral display.

'Oh, it's you again,' she said sourly, to Savage. 'Good morning, Miss Drew. That was a shocking thing that happened last night at your college. Whatever is Brigid Moore coming to, might I ask?'

'Is the Rector in, Margaret? Inspector Savage wishes to see him again.'

The housekeeper set the flowers on a table in the hall. 'No, he's not in. He's over at the Chapel doing a wedding. One of the graduates—ever such a nice boy when he was here. I hope the girl realizes how lucky she is. They're coming in for a cup of tea before going on to the reception. He wants me to meet his bride.'

'How very nice of him.'

'And why shouldn't he be!' demanded Miss Knight. 'I am appreciated sometimes, you know.'

Savage interposed. 'Miss Knight, I was talking to one of your girls just now. We met outside Professor Craske's home.'

'Thelma? What were you talking to her for? I sent her over to clean, not to chat to strangers.'

'I didn't delay her long. She was telling me about finding Mrs Craske in her bath.'

Margaret looked at him sharply. 'What was she saying? She's a flighty, silly sort of girl. I often think the shock of that business made her sillier.'

'She was saying that she only started the cleaning job at the Craskes when you were called away to the country.'

'Yes, that's right. I used to go over and look after Mrs Craske for an hour or so every once in a while. Mind you, only as a favour to her and the Professor. She was always poorly and they knew I'd done a bit of nursing in my time. In fact,' Miss Knight went off on one of her belligerent tangents, 'if it wasn't for all these exams they want you to pass nowadays, I daresay I'd have had my own hospital by now—instead of having what some people like to think is a menial position.'

'I should think being a housekeeper to a University college entails a certain skill for organization, not to mention dedication of spirit,' said Savage pleasantly.

Miss Knight combined an expression of Gilbrethian efficiency with that of a Florence Nightingale. 'You can say that again,' she said, her aggressiveness blunted.

'This call to the country, Miss Knight,' went on Savage persuasively. 'It was on account of some relative's illness, I believe.'

'Yes, my aunty. She took bad and of course they had to send for me at once.'

'What part of the country is that?'

Miss Knight's customary wariness was returning. 'I'd like to know why you're so interested. You've probably never heard of the place. About ten people and a dog live at Audleigh.'

'And when you arrived at Audleigh,' said the inspector conversationally. 'I suppose you found your aunt hale and hearty and the telegram a mistake?'

'Whatever makes you say that?' demanded Miss Knight indignantly. 'Poor Aunty was dead when I got there. I laid her out with my own hands.' She held out her small, strong hands as though they were proof of Aunty's demise.

'I'm sorry,' apologized Savage.

Miss Knight's voice rose. 'There's something queer going on.'

Elizabeth came nobly to Savage's assistance. 'Isn't that your wedding party coming in?' She moved into line with the open front door. 'Yes, here's the Rector.'

Miss Knight's annoyance and suspicion dropped away and her small, round face became wreathed in smiles. She always looked quite girlish when anything pleased her. She whipped off her spotless apron, thrust it into the table drawer, and went to meet the bride and groom.

'Miss Drew, I don't know how I'd manage without you,' said Savage whimsically, as the hall became filled with white satin, morning coats, the scent of gardenias and nuptial gaiety. The Rector, gaunt in cassock and surplice, caught sight of them. He gave a quick nod, then with masterly strategy shepherded the wedding party into one of the parlours. 'I'll be with you in a minute. Margaret will look after you.'

He came towards Savage and Elizabeth, concern in his deep-set eyes. 'They tell me the second missing student committed suicide,' he said, without preamble. 'What is going on at Brigid Moore Hall?'

'I'm endeavouring to find out. Father,' Savage answered quietly. 'There is one point you may be able to help me with. Can you cast your mind back twelve months?'

The Rector nodded. 'And having done so?'

'Mrs Helena Craske, wife of one of the senior lecturers, was found drowned in her bath about that time. The discovery was made by a housemaid from Manning College, part of whose duties at the Craske home seemed to be supervision of the ailing mistress.'

A burst of muffled laughter reached them. The Rector cast a glance at the closed door of the parlour. 'Go on, please, Inspector.'

'On this particular morning, the maid—Thelma Young—was delayed in arriving by a telephone message requesting her to pick up an urgent parcel for the Rector of Manning College at the registrar's office.'

'That is quite correct, Inspector. I recall the incident perfectly. But there was no parcel.'

'How did this incident strike you, Father?'

'It strikes me now that it could have been a hoax.'

A rueful smile touched Savage's mouth. 'I'd rather you said definitely it was a hoax, and that it struck you so at the time.'

The Rector's eyes gleamed in humorous sympathy. 'Not if you want me to be strictly accurate. I have sent one of the maids down to the registrar's office before this. They have also phoned through with a similar message. The only thing that hasn't happened before or since is that there was no parcel.'

'I see,' said Savage slowly, but Elizabeth thought he sounded disappointed.

The gleam in the Rector's deep-set eyes became more pronounced. 'If I were you, Inspector,' he suggested. 'I'd settle for the hoax and work from there.'

'Thanks for the encouragement. Father,' replied Savage ruefully. 'Unfortunately people take exception, not only to being accused of crime, but also to being involved in any way.'

'That is understandable,' agreed the Rector, 'but I really consider that after three—shall I call them tragedies?—the time has come to over-ride sensibilities.'

'Then you do not object to your college being involved?'

'I object very strongly,' replied the Rector calmly. 'But I object even more to whoever is responsible for involving this college.'

13

Clad in a white bathing costume and a scarlet cap, Fiona Searle walked gracefully along the high diving board of the Beaurepaire pool, made a sudden spring and flashed through the air in a neatly executed jack dive. Several tanned young men sitting along the sides exchanged admiring whistles. One of them slipped back into the water. Fiona surfaced to find Peter Baynes alongside, threw out a gay challenge, and with long, rhythmic strokes raced to the end of the pool. There she hauled herself out, and sitting with her scarlet-tipped toes dabbling the water, took off her bright cap.

Young Baynes climbed out after her, 'Hullo!'

'Hullo,' she returned coolly, keeping her face in pert profile.

'That was a terrific dive you did. You're fabulous in the water, Fiona.'

'Why, thanks,' she returned carelessly.

There was a pause, then Peter said, 'Er—how are things?'

'Foul! One of our girls hanged herself last night—so they say.'

'Yes, I know. The Markham girl, wasn't it? I'm terribly sorry.' Then, after a short hesitation, he asked, 'Why did you say that?'

'Say what?'

'That they only say she hanged herself.'

Fiona shrugged irritably. 'I don't know—the whole business stinks. I'd rather not talk about Heather, if you don't mind.'

'Have you been told not to?'

She turned her large eyes on him, but he avoided the gaze. 'No, we haven't been told anything. That's just the trouble. You've no idea what it's like at our college at the moment.' She paused, eyeing him thoughtfully. 'I suppose now you've discovered I can't tell you anything you'll say it's time for lunch.'

'Don't be tough, Fiona,' he muttered. 'You're not the only one finding things foul.'

'Oh? What's on your mind?'

'Everything,' replied Peter, in a suppressed voice. 'A detective type was at Manning last night grilling me about Heather.'

'How grim! Why you?' asked Fiona, puzzled. 'You barely knew her, did you?'

'Because I was weeding your blasted garden in the afternoon and should have stopped her, I suppose. Then that Warden of yours started needling me about the rag. Oh, I had a great time I can tell you—especially with the Rector looking on.'

'So that's where they got to last night! What did Mother Paul say to you?'

Peter shaded his eyes as he gazed across the sun-glinted pool. 'Nothing much, actually.'

'You mean you don't want to tell me,' said Fiona shrewdly. 'Oh, come on—give! You'll feel all the better for it. If you'd just take the trouble to look at me, you'll see my face alive with womanly sympathy.'

He turned his head, an uncertain smile evoked by her words. 'All right. I'll tell you. She asked me, why we didn't stage a rag last year about Hel—Mrs Craske's accident?'

Fiona drew her brows together. 'What a strange thing to say. Mother Paul can't know anything about Helena Craske. Why, that business has been just about forgotten. I wonder what she was driving at.'

'I don't know, but it was beastly being reminded.'

'Yes, you knew Mrs Craske, didn't you?' said Fiona slowly. 'You were one of her pets for a while. Frankly, I can't understand what you could have seen in the woman. She was like a stupid octopus—fastening on to whoever came her way.'

'You're a girl; you wouldn't understand,' he said, in a low voice.

'Oh, she used to try clamping her suckers on Brigid Moore students. She had Nola attached for a while, until I cut her loose.'

'I wish you had done the same for me,' said Peter, and the note of despair in his voice brought a flash of puzzled concern to Fiona's eyes.

'I just wasn't interested in you in those days, ducky,' she replied lightly. 'Anyway, did you want to break loose so badly?'

The boy ran his hand over his crew-cut hair. 'Yes—no! Oh—I don't know. If I'd known what she—but I had no idea—'

'Here, take it easy,' said Fiona kindly. 'If that was the effect

Octopus Helena had on you, I bet you were relieved when she slipped in the bath. I often thought her death must have been a happy release for Professor Craske, but I didn't realize—' Her voice trailed off, and her eyes, once more puzzled and questioning, met the boy's unhappy ones. 'Peter, I don't like this,' she said unsteadily. 'I knew I didn't like it at the beginning, but now I'm simply loathing it.'

'I know what you're thinking,' he said desperately, 'but you're wrong. It's bad enough, but not as bad as that. I didn't make her die deliberately. I never dreamed she meant what she said.'

'What was that? What did she say?'

Peter dropped his head on his chest. 'She said that if I stopped visiting her, she wouldn't be able to face it. You see, I thought I was—was keen on her, and then I realized what a fool I was making of myself—that it was only a stupid phase.'

'Yes, I know,' said Fiona, with slightly scornful tolerance. 'I've heard of boys falling in love with older women. She must have known it was only a phase too.'

'She didn't—at least she pretended she didn't. She said if I stopped coming to see her, she couldn't bear it. And she kept on hinting at committing suicide.'

There was silence between the boy and girl sitting on the edge of the pool with the shouts and laughter and splashes about them. Presently Fiona gave a little shiver. 'Disgusting!' she said, in a low voice. 'But even if she did commit suicide, it's not your fault, Peter.'

'Then why did your Warden bring it up last night—in front of that detective too? What is going on at your college?'

Fiona raised her head and looked about her. 'I don't know. No one knows, except maybe the Warden and Miss Drew. But I can tell you who's at the bottom of it, who started it all. That red-haired little so-and-so over there.'

'Who? Oh, that kid. The one whose sister did a bunk! She was at Manning last night too.' He gave a weary, sidelong glance. 'Fiona, it's been great talking to you. I feel loads better. I know you won't let on to anyone.'

Fiona gazed across at Judith Mornane, a speculative spark in her eyes. 'No, I won't say anything,' she promised absently.

'Do you think you can try and find out what's happening?' asked

Peter. 'This being in the dark is pure hell.'

Fiona stretched her cap between her hands and put it on. 'I'll try. I'll let you know if I hear anything.'

'Why are you looking so mad? Is it because of what I told you about Mrs Craske and me?'

'No, not you. I just feel mad,' returned Fiona, through clenched teeth. She lowered herself into the water, then looked up as Peter called her name. 'What is it?'

'I think you're the most, Fiona! If there's anything I can do—when are you having your Stunt Nite? I've got the most terrific film if you'd like me to bring over my projector—candid shots and such like from last year. There are one or two beauties with you in them. And maybe the Mornane girl would like to see her long-lost sister.'

Fiona grabbed the rail. 'You mean you've got a shot of Maureen Mornane?'

'I think so—in a crowd scene outside Wilson Hall. One of the chaps spotted a girl with a limp when I was running it through in my room last night.'

Fiona thought for a moment. 'I'll take you up on that offer,' she said, letting go the rail. 'I'd better go now. See you!'

The boy watched her lithe, white-clad figure cut swiftly through the water.

Judith was enjoying the combination of cool water and hot sun, idly kicking her legs as she clung to the side of the pool. She was thinking, not unhappily, of the dam at home where she and Maureen used to bathe.

'Can you swim, Judith?' asked a crisp voice, close by.

She saw Fiona and replied warily, 'A little. I can stay afloat.'

'I'm relieved to hear you say so,' returned the other, her eyes alight with part mischief, part malice. 'I wouldn't like you to accuse me directly of murder.'

Before Judith knew what she was about, Fiona seized her by one ankle and with a sudden jerk tipped her neatly head first into the water. She came up spluttering and indignant, but Fiona was no longer anywhere to be seen.

The ducking was part of a bout of persecution. The sudden and hideous death of one of their fellow-students had unconsciously inspired in the girls of Brigid Moore Hall a desire for a scapegoat. To them, Judith Mornane was the cause of their present distress, which they sought to alleviate by pinpricking tactics. Soup was spilled over her gown at lunch, her bedroom door became mysteriously jammed and the chair she chose in the recreation room suddenly collapsed under her weight.

Both Elizabeth and Miss Dove guessed what was afoot, but lack of evidence and inclination prevented their doing anything. They too felt resentful. However, it wasn't long before the Warden realized the state of affairs.

Going upstairs later in the day, she found Judith, wearing only a cotton dressing-gown, crouched behind the banisters on the landing.

'How odd!' Mother Paul exclaimed mildly. 'But I daresay you have some reason, Judith.'

The girl cast a quick glance into the hall below, flushed scarlet, and tried in vain to hide the large pitcher of water behind her.

The Warden's thoughtful gaze took in the scene. 'What is the trouble, child?' But Judith muttered unintelligibly. 'Have those naughty girls been teasing you again? You'd better tell me. We don't want matters to get out of hand. I daresay they consider you are to blame for poor Heather Markham.'

'And I am—I am!' burst out Judith, with a passionate contrition. 'Oh, Mother Paul, what a mess I started!'

'You did indeed, dear,' agreed the Warden candidly. 'What are you intending to do with that jug of water?'

A martial light returned to Judith's eyes. 'I wanted to give Fiona and Nola a taste of their own medicine. I can take a certain amount, especially when I realize how much to blame I am, but not—not itching powder.'

'What is that, dear?' asked the Warden conversationally. 'It sounds quite horrid.'

'The last straw!' replied Judith tragically. 'All down my back and then the bathrooms upstairs were locked. Fiona's work of course. Miss Drew sent me over to the Cottage to use theirs, and while I was having a shower someone took my clothes.'

Mother Paul looked thoughtful. Suddenly she went to the balustrade.

'Nola! Fiona!' she called, as the two girls came in the front door. They were sharing the same yards-long colourful scarf and laughing at each other.

'Yes, Reverend Mother?' They advanced obediently, faces upturned.

'Now!' whispered Mother Paul, stepping back. 'And see that you clear up any mess, Judith.'

She glided quickly up the stairs without a backward glance. Only when the sound of a fluid thud, followed by gasps of protestation floated up did she check her step.

'I really shouldn't have abetted it. What would Mother Tobias say if she knew?' she murmured to herself.

'Such a day it has been!' reported Miss Dove at supper. 'People mean well of course, but it seems to me that their curiosity is greater than their sympathy. Even Professor Whipple stopped me as I passed their place on the way home. He wanted to know if the police were still haunting our threshold. Don't ask me, I told him, Miss Drew is the person best qualified to answer that question.'

Elizabeth felt the sidelong glance and realized her colleague was feeling some sort of perverted jealousy.

'I suppose your calling in this morning to tell the Whipples about Heather prompted Professor Whipple's curiosity,' she countered.

'Well, naturally—when he knew his wife had been questioned by that inspector from Russell Street. It seems to me that our worthy Warden is positively encouraging that unfeeling policeman to embarrass people. I believe he was all over the University today asking questions and taking notes—though about what I am sure I cannot tell you.'

Elizabeth went on buttering bread. 'I believe Heather's father was here this afternoon,' she remarked presently, hoping to ease the constraint. 'Was he very upset?'

The Science tutor speared a piece of bread. 'He seemed more dazed than upset. I told him everything I could without descending to the macabre. But—my goodness—if he had only seen his daughter as she looked when I opened that cupboard door!'

'What did make you open that door?' asked Elizabeth suddenly.

Miss Dove searched for her table napkin. 'I told you—my gown. I'd mislaid it.'

'Your gown was on your bed all the time.'

The Science tutor held the napkin to her flushed face. 'I told Mr Markham that time was a great healer and that the sharp edge of his sorrow would become blunted as years went on.'

'You were not looking for your gown.'

'Never mind what I was looking for,' said Miss Dove sharply. 'It's what I found that was of dreadful importance.'

'Then you admit you told Inspector Savage an untruth.'

Miss Dove blinked her eyes rapidly. 'Really, Miss Drew! I can only say I take strong exception to your manner. Your attitude is, no doubt, a result of your consorting with that policeman all the morning. You're not suggesting, I hope, that I already knew poor Heather had used the locker in which to hang herself.'

'I'm not suggesting anything,' replied the girl steadily, 'but should the police query your reason for opening the locker, I think you should have a truthful reply ready.'

'And why should they query me?' demanded Miss Dove cutting bread and jam with vicious little strokes. 'What is happening here? In these suicide cases they don't usually stay around worrying people.'

She paused and then went on in a higher voice, 'It's not fair that we should all be upset like this. Look at the students for instance— they know there's an atmosphere of tension in the house. They don't bicker and play nasty tricks as a rule. The way they've been treating that Mornane girl—not that everything is not her fault. If it hadn't been for her—'

'Be quiet!' whispered Elizabeth urgently. 'They're looking at you.'

Miss Dove strove to calm herself. 'I don't know what came over me,' she muttered, putting down her knife with trembling fingers. 'I hope you will forget the lapse, Miss Drew.'

'Of course,' said Elizabeth automatically. 'Would you like another cup of tea?'

'That would be kind of you.'

Elizabeth rose and took their cups to the side table where the urn stood. When she came back, the Science tutor said in an embarrassed voice, 'Honesty is the best policy. It wasn't strictly the truth—about looking for my gown in the cupboard. But I don't see that it matters.'

'No, I shouldn't think it would matter,' agreed Elizabeth soothingly. 'More sugar?'

'Thank you. I remembered noticing a raincoat in the locker belonging to Professor Craske. He must have left it there some time when he was using our lecture room. I decided to return it to him. Naturally, what I found first wiped all thought of raincoats out of my head. There seemed no point in dragging Professor Craske's name into Heather's tragedy. After all, I could quite easily have been looking for my gown.'

Elizabeth frowned. She had a mental picture of the untidy Craske living-room, and a plastic raincoat newly slung across Helena Craske's couch. 'But you have since returned the coat?' she asked slowly.

'Why, no! As a matter of fact, when I looked this morning it had gone. I daresay Professor Craske must have picked it up himself.'

There was a pause. Elizabeth pushed her chair away from the table and rose. 'Yes, that is probably what happened. Will you excuse me now? I'll see you later in the Cottage.'

'How odd!' said the Warden, pacing to and fro as far as the confines of her office would allow. Elizabeth, sitting in the only other chair, had to move her knees sideways each time the nun passed. 'Why should Miss Dove suddenly take it into her head to look for Professor Craske's raincoat at nine o'clock on a fine night? And why should she feel the necessity of keeping his name out of things?'

She paused in her perambulations, took out her notebook, frowned at its pages, then asked abruptly, 'Does Miss Dove suspect the strong probability of Heather having been murdered?'

Elizabeth shook her head. 'I don't think so—yet. But Inspector Savage's presence is causing concern.'

'One has a certain instinct when all is not well,' said the Warden thoughtfully, 'which is probably what led Miss Dove into telling an untruth. But why should she be so concerned about protecting Professor Craske?'

Elizabeth stared down at her hands without replying. She was feeling all the discomfiture of an unwilling informer.

The nun stopped in front of her. 'Have I said something odd,

Elizabeth? Don't you find it puzzling too?'

The girl answered awkwardly .'Well, not exactly. You haven't yet met Professor Craske, have you? He is very—very good-looking and wom—I mean, people—find him very charming.'

'Do you, dear?' asked the nun, with embarrassing simplicity.

'I am engaged to Dr Bertram,' replied Elizabeth coldly.

'Ah, yes! Such a nice open face. Not good-looking perhaps, but most devoted to you, dear. I promised not to let any harm befall you.'

Elizabeth sat up. 'Timothy has been speaking to you?' The Warden looked a little abashed. 'Oh dear, and I promised not to tell you. He is worried about this dreadful business we are caught up in. He seems to consider we set about becoming involved deliberately. Quite put-out he was, poor man! I did my best to convey the inevitableness of our positions, but he went away still looking rather—I'm afraid I can only describe his demeanour as—cross.'

'Well, never mind about Timothy now. He had no right to come worrying you. I'll speak to him.'

The Warden regarded her doubtfully. 'I'm sure you know how to manage your private affairs, dear, but—however, to return to Miss Dove. Are she and Professor Craske planning to be married too?'

Elizabeth wriggled under the candid gaze. 'I don't think so.'

Mother Paul pondered for a moment. 'You mean it is a one-sided affair?' she inquired. 'Oh, poor Miss Dove! Tell me, Elizabeth—would you say that this charming, good-looking professor is a—flirt?'

Elizabeth could not help smiling at the effort with which the nun brought out the word.

'Professor Craske certainly delights in being agreeable to any member of the opposite sex,' she admitted.

'Any member? Even if they are cross-eyed or lame, or perhaps engaged, even married?'

Elizabeth wriggled anew. 'Really, I—'

'Yes, dear, I know,' interrupted the Warden apologetically. You don't want to shock me, and instead I am shocking you. But you must realize how very inexperienced I am in such matters. Whom else can I ask?'

Elizabeth had a wild vision of Mother Paul discussing romantic love with her community. 'Of course you may ask me anything,' she replied, rather unsteadily. 'I'm sorry I'm being so clumsy-tongued. Yes, Professor Craske is an out-and-out—flirt. Being engaged or even married is no deterrent, but whether he realizes his attentions are sometimes taken seriously, or wants them to be, I do not know.'

The nun was silent again. Presently she said mildly, 'It seems strange that he has shown no indication of wishing to remarry. What is stopping him, I wonder? Is he so content in his present way of life? Or—is he afraid?'

'Afraid?' queried Elizabeth, amused. 'Really, Mother Paul! Why should he be afraid?'

'I don't know,' replied the Warden slowly. 'But I can't help thinking he might be.'

Elizabeth stared at her with some exasperation, wondering what extraordinary notions she was turning over in her shrewd yet child-like mind.

'Mother Paul, you seem to know more about us all than we do ourselves. Even Inspector Savage is inclined to think so. He instructed me to tell you about his inquiries this morning. He is most anxious for you to confide your suspicions frankly to him.'

The nun said meekly. 'I'm afraid I'm a sad trial to that good man.'

She sat down at her desk, folded her hands under her scapular and fixed attentive eyes on the girl, who proceeded to relate carefully the events of the morning.

When the story came to an end, the Warden remained silent and thoughtful. Presently she made a note or two in her book, then regarded the result gravely.

'Yes, I feel sure I am right. But I would like something a little more conclusive. I cannot present a theory to Inspector Savage with only the flimsiest evidence to support it. It is so odd that even I have difficulty in believing it sometimes,' she added naïvely. She heard a smothered sigh and reached over to press Elizabeth's hand contritely. 'And a sad trial to you too, dear.'

'You needn't worry about me, Mother Paul. But what I am concerned about is the students. This atmosphere of uncertainty and tension is no good for them.'

'Oh, dear, are they still being difficult? It's only because they're unhappy, you know.'

'Then something had better be done about bringing lightness and joy into their lives,' advised Elizabeth dryly. 'Unless you want their unhappiness to deteriorate into straight-out viciousness.'

'Yes, they want something to take their minds off poor Heather. Can you suggest anything, Elizabeth?'

'Perhaps you could bring their Stunt Nite forward. They usually enjoy that. It was due in another week or two anyway.'

'What is a Stunt Nite? Oh dear, it is sometimes difficult being new to one's task. Though wait! I remember dear Mother Raphael's writing something in the procedure she left for my guidance. So considerate!'

The Warden selected a thick folder from the desk and put on her spectacles again. 'Yes, here it is! *A mid-term festival for students, designed for relief from close study—taking the form of a concert and supper wholly organized by the students and presented to the community and staff of Brigid Moore Hall and such guests as invited by the Warden. No trousers to be worn.* She glanced up, asking mildly. 'Does that mean no male guests, Elizabeth?'

The girl bit her lip to prevent a smile. 'I think Mother Raphael was referring to the costumes worn in the concert.

But as a rule, we don't have outsiders. The girls prefer it that way. They think up skits and put on musical items of college interest only. Oh, and you have to allow them free run of the kitchen. You've no idea the messes they concoct for supper.'

The Warden beamed happily and closed the folder. 'The very thing! How long do they take to prepare for their Stunt Nite?'

'No time at all. In fact, the more unrehearsed and spontaneous the better they like it.'

14

'Just as though we were children,' said Nola angrily, pacing up and down the recreation room, 'to be diverted by a treat.'

'And a jolly good idea too,' retorted Monica. 'Maybe you girls are bursting with curiosity as to what is going on, but I'd rather not know, thanks. I came to Brigid Moore to do Medicine, not to get involved in anything shady. As far as I'm concerned the Warden's all right.'

'Oh, you!' exclaimed Nola, pausing and rattling her gold chain bracelet impatiently. 'All you're interested in is study, study, study! How can you keep your nose in a book all the time as though one of us committed suicide every week, I don't know.'

'It helps me forget Heather,' returned Monica gruffly. 'And if you had any sense you'd do the same. Or at least follow the Warden's lead without question.'

Nola swung round. 'Supposing we try pumping Learned Liz? She was with that inspector all the morning. She must know what's going on. What do you say, Fiona?'

Fiona was seated at the table in the centre of the room engaged in experimenting with different shades and textures of nail polish.

She gave a shrug. 'We wouldn't get any change out of Learned Liz any more than the Warden.' She held up a wet forefinger nail and inspected it closely. 'I vote we concentrate on Stunt Nite as Monica says. You never know what might be the outcome of that.'

Nola looked down at her doubtfully. 'Are you planning a skit along the lines of the Manning rag? Is that what you mean?'

Fiona wiped her forefinger clean with a piece of tissue and selected another colour varnish. 'No, not a skit.'

'What, then?' asked Nola, puzzled.

Fiona replied airily, 'Oh, a song and dance act. A jazz number of the 'twenties. Come in on it with me. We'll dress up in short skirts and long beads and do the Charleston.'

'That sounds terrific! I'll be with you. But what did you mean—?'

'Let's start practising now,' interrupted Fiona, jumping up. 'Will someone play the piano for us while we work out a routine?'

'Can't you use the parlour piano?' one of the students objected. 'Some of us want to work on a charade. We want a bit of quiet for the Muse to start operating.'

'All right,' agreed Fiona easily. 'Come on, Nola, we'll go into the parlour.'

They took with them a Conservatorium student who was prepared to bang out jazz for as long as they heeded the pained expression on her face. 'Fiona, what are you cooking up?' asked Nola suspiciously. 'I bet it's something more than a song and dance routine.'

Fiona's eyes gleamed and a little excited smile played at one corner of her mouth. 'I don't know yet. But whatever happens, it is going to pay for that drenching we received this afternoon.'

'Judy Mornane?'

'Yes, young Judith—oh, and our enterprising Warden too.'

'You'd better lay off, Fiona,' said the music student uneasily. 'What's the use of carrying things on?'

Fiona paused, one hand on the parlour door knob. The look of mischief had left her face. 'I'm not too sure that it won't be quite a deal of use,' she said slowly. 'Listen, you two! We know that something's wrong here at B.M. but we don't know what. I know for a fact that the—the wrongness—isn't just isolated to our college. It's other places in the University—Manning, for example.'

'How do you know that?'

'One of the Manning boys told me at the pool today. It's all tied up somehow—Maureen Mornane's disappearance, Heather and—well I just can't tell you about the other trouble. I promised I wouldn't and anyway it's rather foul.'

'What Manning boy were you speaking to?'

'Peter Baynes,' replied Fiona. 'You asked me what I was cooking up. I'll tell you. Peter has a movie reel he has promised to bring over and show us for Stunt Nite. He took it last year during Orientation week. One of the shots includes Maureen Mornane.'

The other girls regarded her in silence. Then Nola said slowly, 'Judith is not going to like that.'

'I don't like it either,' said the music student frankly. 'And it wasn't my sister who disappeared. Fiona, I think you're starting something you haven't the slightest idea how to handle.'

The wicked smile returned to Fiona's face as she turned the door handle. 'Maybe, but you didn't get a pail of water tipped over you, with the Warden's tacit approval.' She stopped on the threshold of the parlour. 'Oh, I didn't know the parlour was occupied. Do you mind if we come in? We want to practise for Stunt Nite.'

'Speak of the devil,' muttered Nola, as Judith Mornane rose quickly from a chair in the corner where she had been reading.

'Yes, come in. I was just going anyway.'

'Stay if you like,' suggested Fiona carelessly.

'What are you looking so scared about?' asked Nola. 'We haven't come to lynch you, even though you did win the last round.'

'What Nola means is that we've retired from the lists,' exclaimed Fiona. 'The honours of the battle are all yours.'

'Now, now!' said the music student uneasily. 'I won't play for you two if you're going to gang up again. I hate rows.'

'Yes, let's forget it,' said Fiona winningly. She could be very attractive when she liked. 'Stay and be our audience, Judith.'

The flush deepened on the younger girl's face. 'Why, thank you,' she stammered. 'I would like to watch.'

Casting a look of deepest suspicion at her two companions, the music student went to the piano. Soon they were wrangling cheerfully about cues and dance steps, all thought of past feuding apparently forgotten.

'Really an excellent notion,' the Warden told Elizabeth the next day, coming across her in the Cottage reading-room. 'I am most grateful to you. Everyone is so happy and occupied. Poor Sister Lydia—such odd things going on in the kitchen too!'

'Well, don't say I didn't warn you,' returned Elizabeth, after working out what the Warden was talking about. The nun's habit of making naïve and impetuous observations without mentioning the subject matter never failed to amuse her. But her smile faded. 'I wish I could share your optimism, Mother Paul. I can't help feeling we're in for something.'

'Oh? What sort of feeling, dear?'

'Everyone seems a mite too merry and matey,' said Elizabeth, troubled. 'Even young Judith has been drawn into the fun. It's my belief Fiona Searle is responsible for her sudden popularity, and, from experience, whatever that girl does she has some reason.'

'I understand what you mean. However, there's no point in meeting trouble half-way.' She took up a book idly, avoiding the girl's gaze. 'Which puts me in mind of a little matter I wanted to consult you about, Elizabeth.'

'Oh? What is that?' asked Elizabeth warily.

Mother Paul shot a precautionary glance about the room, then put down the book. 'In regard to Professor Craske's raincoat which Miss Dove intended returning—presumably as an excuse to call next door. Now you said you saw it in his living-room. Are you quite certain of that?'

'Yes, quite certain.'

'Then just how and when did it get there?'

'He must have come in and collected it,' said Elizabeth uncertainly.

'But why should Professor Craske, in the midst of this fine warm weather, remember a raincoat which had been in that locker for some time—probably from some wet day last term when he was here to lecture? Don't you find that curious, Elizabeth?'

'I daresay there is some quite simple explanation.'

The Warden beamed. 'Of course—and I knew I could rely on you, dear. Not a pleasant task, for I know you are not easy in Professor Craske's company. But you need not stay long.'

'Stay long where?' demanded Elizabeth, with foreboding. 'What are you talking about?'

'Just a little call next door,' said the Warden coaxingly. 'I want you to try and find out how the raincoat got back to its owner.'

Elizabeth looked uncomfortable. 'Are you sure that's necessary? I—I told you about Professor Craske, the way he— He'll probably start thinking that I—' Her discomfiture increased as she met the nun's limpid eyes. She searched wildly for a good excuse and thought of what Timothy would say if he knew his fiancée intended seeing a man with a reputation like Craske's alone in his house. The situation between them had already deteriorated enough. Ever since Timothy's return, they had been, as it were, out of tune with each other, and now, man-like, he was making a ridiculous issue out of her being embroiled in an affair which he kept pointing out the police would be quite capable of handling alone.

She had seen him that morning in the Anthropological museum which was situated on the top floor of the Considine building. She was feeling rather annoyed that he had been to see the Warden, and this unfortunately spoiled her intention of trying to explain the situation into which she had been unwillingly dragged. He had taken her to lunch at the Union, where a further exchange of strictures between them had almost ended in a quarrel.

Mother Paul surveyed her anxiously. 'It's not just the raincoat, Elizabeth, but—no, I'd better not say any more just now. Will you do this little task for me?'

'Oh, all right,' said the girl ungraciously. 'I'll go in and see Professor Craske after supper.'

The Warden looked both relieved and guilty. 'You must wonder at my asking you to behave so unconventionally, especially after my promise to Dr Bertram.'

'I'm not afraid of either Richard Craske or Timothy,' said Elizabeth haughtily.

'No, of course not, dear, but—' Mother Paul fingered another book. 'You must forgive my prying, Elizabeth, but have you quarrelled with Dr Bertram?'

Elizabeth gave a short laugh. 'Unfortunately, no! There was the possibility of a fine air-clearing row this morning, but it just didn't come off.'

The nun turned away. 'Oh, dear, I feel so dreadful about this,' she murmured.

'The trouble with Timothy,' went on Elizabeth, clenching her teeth as she warmed to the subject, 'is that he badly needs a jolt—a big jolt. You know we've been engaged for nearly two years, Mother Paul? It's humiliating! I want to get married before he goes on this winter expedition of his to the Centre, but he won't hear of it.' She looked across at the nun. 'Mother Paul, I don't want to marry anyone else but Tim. I can't break our engagement when I don't mean it. What am I going to do?'

The Warden blinked at this outburst from her usually reserved Humanities tutor. 'You said something about a big jolt,' she said timidly. 'If there was some way to inflict that jolt, would you do so?'

'Willingly,' replied Elizabeth bitterly. 'If you can think of a way. I'll be only too pleased to follow it.'

Mother Paul gave her a long, searching look. 'Such a relief to hear you say so, dear. I didn't care for the notion of interfering, but I could see how very unsatisfactory the situation was between you. As Miss Dove would say, it will now be a matter of killing two birds with the one stone.' But Elizabeth was too taken up with thinking dark, frustrated thoughts of Timothy to pay close heed. It was only later at supper, when Miss Dove uttered another ornithological proverb, that she felt a vague uneasiness and wondered what the Warden had meant.

'Fine feathers make fine birds,' remarked the Science tutor, eyeing Elizabeth's full-skirted, flower-patterned frock. 'I take it you are going out tonight.'

Elizabeth realized her mistake in putting on this dress which she had selected deliberately as pleasing to Craske's eyes. She should have left changing until later. 'Yes, I'm going out for a short while—just visiting.'

'With a devoted swain, I suppose?'

She felt a rising irritation. What business was it of Miss Dove's where or with whom she went? Then mindful of just whom she was going to visit and how much Miss Dove might consider it her business, she said lightly. 'If he can make it. He's pretty busy at the moment.' She finished her supper hastily so as to avoid further questioning.

Out in the hall, she picked up the fluffy stole she had hidden in the hall-stand, wrapped it about her shoulders and then quietly left the house. She felt strangely elated and reckless, as though she were breaking some code of behaviour and found the process stimulating. But not so reckless as to be unmindful of some discretion. She knew it would be better if she were not seen entering the house next door, so she wandered slowly down the street, waiting for daylight to fade.

'Miss Drew!' called a voice quietly. 'I would like a word with you.'

She looked up to find herself outside the Whipple residence and Professor Whipple at the other side of the fence. Here was an excellent opportunity, not only to kill time, but to use as a cover. If need be, she could let it be known that she had been visiting the Whipples. 'Certainly, Dean,' she replied, going towards the gate.

He hurried forward and put a hand on the latch. 'No, please don't come in. I—I'd rather my wife didn't know.'

'Very well,' agreed Elizabeth quietly. 'What is it you want?'

He spoke with difficulty, without his usual manner of ironical benevolence. 'I heard—that is, my wife tells me you are on friendly terms with a police inspector from Russell Street.'

'I know Inspector Savage, but I am not on friendly terms with him.'

*At any rate you were in his company for the greater part of the other morning,' said the Dean hastily. 'You took him to see Professor Craske and then on to Manning College to the Rector.'

Inspector Savage requested me to go with him.'

'Oh, quite—quite! I would like to know the purpose of these visits, Miss Drew.'

Elizabeth regarded him searchingly. 'Why?' she asked bluntly.

Professor Whipple looked away, trying to laugh. 'I had an interview with Inspector Savage myself. He came to see me in my study after lunch.'

'Then why didn't you ask him the purposes of his various calls?'

'I —I didn't quite understand why he wanted to see me.'

'Surely he made the purpose of that call clear?'

'No—no! In fact, I told him frankly I failed to understand what he was driving at, and the interview ended somewhat ambiguously. But there was a vague mention about a—red-haired girl from your college who disappeared last year.'

'Anything else?' asked Elizabeth, as he hesitated.

'Yes—yes, he said something about Helena—Professor Craske's late wife, you know.'

Elizabeth was silent, wondering what was best said and best left unsaid. At last she asked carefully. 'You want me to tell you just what it is Inspector Savage knows—is that it?'

'I'm not asking you to betray any confidence,' he said hurriedly. 'But—but there is an uncertainty about things at the moment which is—Miss Drew, I must know why that inspector is here and what he wants! In fact, I insist upon your telling me!' He drew out his handkerchief, passed it across his forehead, then pressed it against his lips.

Elizabeth's heart beat fast. She was not used to evading issues with

Deans of Faculties. 'Inspector Savage was called by the Warden because one of our girls committed suicide.'

'Yes, yes. A tragic business. Most distressing for you all at Brigid Moore. But why should your Warden call in a man who, from what I've heard, usually investigates criminal cases?'

'Mother Paul has some acquaintance with him,' said Elizabeth steadily.

'Indeed? Rather a strange acquaintance—a nun and a police inspector. How did the Warden happen to know him?'

'Oh, I don't know,' said Elizabeth, deliberately vague. 'It's surprising the number and variety of people nuns can come into contact with.'

'Then this Inspector Savage is, in effect, here at your Warden's special request?'

Elizabeth felt caught. 'Inspector Savage is interested in the suicide note Heather Markham left. There was some reference in it to the disappearance of the red-haired student you mentioned earlier.'

'Yes, yes, I know all that,' he said, impatiently. 'It seems absurd if, after a whole year, the police have suddenly decided to put further investigations into operation. What has prompted this move?'

Elizabeth thought for a moment, wondering if Savage would mind her taking a bold step. 'This move was prompted by the possibility of Maureen Mornane having been seen leaving the Craske place on the morning of Mrs Craske's accident.'

'What? What?' he exclaimed. 'Who could possibly have seen her leaving? No one would have been about at that particular time.'

'Miss Dove thinks she saw her—from the laboratory window in the Cottage.'

'Miss Dove? Then she—' he broke off and made as though to turn away.

'Just a moment!' said Elizabeth quietly. 'Why were you so sure no one could have seen Maureen leaving the Craskes'? And how do you know at what particular time it was?'

The Dean paused. Suddenly he came back to the gate and gripped his hands on the pickets. 'I know, Miss Drew, because I too happened to see a red-haired girl on the day Helena Craske died. Miss Dove was quite right.'

'You saw Maureen coming out of the Craskes' place?' She saw a gleam of his characteristic ironical smile through the gloom.

'No, Miss Drew. The other way round. Maureen saw me leaving the Craske house.'

15

Professor Whipple's words seemed to hang on the soft still evening air. Elizabeth knew what he had admitted was important and that it was up to her to take full advantage of the admission. There was no Warden or Inspector Savage at hand.

'Why are you telling me this?'

His reply came quietly. 'Call it laying my cards on the table—in the hope that you will do the same.'

'What makes you think I have a hand to display?'

'You know what is in your Warden's hand,' he said quickly.

'But you said you were not asking me to betray any confidence,' countered the girl, surprised by her own skill at evasion.

The Dean was silent. Suddenly a voice called from nearby. 'Eddie, where are you? Eddie!'

'I'll go if you like,' murmured Elizabeth.

'You needn't bother,' he said wearily. 'Actually my wife knows everything. I just didn't want to worry her any more. I'm at the gate. Ruby, talking to Miss Drew.'

Mrs Whipple's larger figure loomed alongside her husband. 'What are you talking to her for? Eddie, what have you been saying?' She pushed him aside and addressed Elizabeth menacingly. 'What have you been nagging about? I won't have my husband being worried by the likes of you.' She sounded more common than ever, as though she was using her earthy plain-speaking as a weapon.

'Professor Whipple asked to speak to me.'

'Yes, that's perfectly true. Ruby. I wanted to find out if Miss Drew knew what was happening. I told her that the Mornane girl saw me leaving Helena's place.'

'Eddie, you fool!' exclaimed Mrs Whipple. 'Do you know what you've done? Didn't I tell you this girl is the one who was with that policeman?'

'Does it matter?' he asked, in a defeated way.

'Of course it matters. You can't afford any scandal in your

position.' She waited for him to speak, but when he stood silent and bowed she turned to Elizabeth again. 'Well, if Eddie's not prepared to fight, I am. So you can just listen to me, Miss Drew. You're to forget anything Eddie said—see? He was nowhere near Helena Craske's house the day she died, so he couldn't have seen any student from Brigid Moore—red-haired or otherwise. We were both at our cottage down the Bay. We hadn't come back here because I was sick, and Eddie was looking after me. And I'm prepared to swear to that until the last breath I take.'

'Then you'll do your husband immeasurable harm,' said Elizabeth quietly. 'It is already a well-known fact that he was with Professor Craske when Miss Dove broke the news about the Professor's wife.'

'Eddie only came up for a short visit—to see how things were getting on without him. You can't count that.'

Professor Whipple put a hand on his wife's arm. 'My dear, I do appreciate your loyalty. Heavens knows I don't deserve it. But you are being a little foolish.'

'You took the late train,' she declared fiercely. 'You couldn't have got to the University before Helena died.'

'Yes, I told you I took the late train. Ruby, but what time did I leave the cottage?'

'You said you wanted to have a swim first, that you would go straight from the beach to catch the train.'

'And that night you asked me why I hadn't been for a swim. Don't you remember? You noticed my trunks and towel were dry.'

'Eddie, Eddie! Don't be a fool!' she almost moaned. 'Don't give away more than you have to.'

'It's too late. Ruby. My conscience has never been completely at ease since Helena died.'

'Oh, Eddie!' said Mrs Whipple, and sank her head with its clusters of dyed curls on his shoulder.

'Supposing you tell me precisely what is troubling you,' suggested Elizabeth awkwardly. 'I may be able to help. It's true that I know Inspector Savage fairly well. I'm sure he will listen to me and believe what I say. You came up early that day in order to see Mrs Craske, is that it, Dean?'

Mrs Whipple raised her head to exclaim venomously, 'That

creature! This is all her fault. I'll swear she did it on purpose, just to ruin Eddie.'

'Hush, Ruby, hush! She was ill; she didn't know what she was doing. Yes, I wanted to see Helena, Miss Drew.' He bent his head again, his voice constrained. 'I don't know how much of this got around the University. I suppose there were rumours. I have to confess that there was a short—a very short space of time when I felt a—a certain sympathetic devotion to Helena Craske.'

'Sympathetic fiddlesticks!' exclaimed Mrs Whipple, with a harsh laugh. 'She had you hooked good and proper. Helena Craske was nothing short of a nymphomaniac, Miss Drew. She'd try and seduce anyone who came near enough to her precious invalid couch.'

'Ruby, you're not to talk like that. I told you nothing happened between us.'

'It would have been a sight more healthy if it had,' she retorted. 'But that was Helena for you—leading people on to breaking point, squeezing the last drops out of them. How I hated her when I saw what she was doing to you!'

'Why did you want to see Mrs Craske, Dean?' asked Elizabeth quietly.

'To say good-bye—for the last time. You see I'd tried to—to free myself before, but she—she just wouldn't let go. It was so awkward—living next door and Richard Craske being a personal friend.'

'Did Professor Craske know what was happening?'

'Of course he did!' stated Mrs Whipple forthrightly. 'He'd seen the same thing happen so many times. There was nothing he could do—Helena never did anything actually wrong. She was always the sweet, clinging, invalid, desperate for affection—the bitch!'

'Ruby, Ruby!'

'Oh, I could have killed her!' Mrs Whipple thumped her closed fist on the gate.

'Don't say things like that, Mrs Whipple.' said Elizabeth sharply. 'Please go on, Dean.'

'I had arranged to call on her in the morning at a time when I knew there wouldn't be anyone about to see me. I found her in the living-room. She was wearing a dressing-gown and lying on her couch. I told her straight out that I was seeing her for the last time.

And then—' he paused.

'Go on.'

'Oh, she put on a frightful scene.' Professor Whipple dabbed his face again at the memory. 'It was most unnerving. I didn't know what to do, whether to call a doctor or to—but that is by the way. What she said was far worse—that she would take her own life if I didn't keep up our—our friendship. I tried to reason with her, to comfort her, but she—she kept clinging to me and wanting me to promise to keep seeing her. When I told her my decision was final, she said again that she would commit suicide. I thought she was merely distraught, and that there was nothing more that I could do. I left the house and then it was, as I was closing the gate, that I saw the student from Brigid Moore. She had just come out of her own gate, and was walking towards me.'

'And you think she recognized you?'

Whipple said bitterly, 'From the way she stared and then ran back to her college—yes. I crossed the road to the University gates as quickly as I could. I didn't dare look back.'

Elizabeth was silent. There was some point in the Dean's story that she could not quite grasp—something essential that was evading her.

Professor Whipple was speaking again. 'That threat to take her own life was the last I heard from Helena. I was with Richard in my study a little more than an hour later when Miss Dove came to break the news of her death. You can imagine what my feelings were, Miss Drew—what they have been ever since, in fact. It was only because of Richard's more noticeable distress that I was able to disguise my own.'

Elizabeth looked up. 'Professor Craske was genuinely concerned then? And yet you said, Mrs Whipple, that he knew what type of woman his wife was.'

He must have known,' she retorted defiantly. 'Dick Craske's no fool, even if he might have been complaisant.'

'Then you never actually heard him complain about his wife?'

'Not in so many words—no,' she returned grudgingly.

Now, that is what Mother Paul would call odd, reflected Elizabeth. Why was Richard Craske so upset by the news of his wife's death when evidence shows that she was continually playing him false?

Aloud she said, 'I will tell Inspector Savage about your story, if that is what you want, Dean. You may be quite certain that if he does act upon it in any way, it will be with the greatest caution and consideration.'

'Thank you, Miss Drew, thank you! But can't you tell me anything further—just what Inspector Savage has in mind? I feel—in fact, quite a number of people feel—that something is being held back.'

Again Elizabeth tried to think of the right words, 'Mrs Whipple said something about scandal,' she said hesitantly. 'No one can afford scandal, least of all a University.'

'You do believe Eddie yourself, don't you, Miss Drew?' asked Mrs Whipple.

'Oh, yes—yes, of course!' Elizabeth tried to reply without hesitation. 'I must go now. Please don't worry. I'm sure everything is going to be all right.' Without waiting for their misgivings to grow into questions, she turned and hurried into the dark.

She was already shaken by the time she reached the Craske gate, but she trod resolutely up the path. The front door was ajar to allow a draught to enter the house after the warm day, but she rang at the bell and went to wait on the porch edge with her back turned.

The porch light went on. 'And what fair visitor have I tonight?' asked Richard Craske's mocking voice suddenly, making her jump. 'Why, Elizabeth! What a delightful surprise. But wait! Don't tell me! You've brought a watchdog with you.'

She came forward, forcing a smile and allowing her fluffy stole to slip away from her shoulders.

'No chaperon this time. I was out for a stroll, saw your light and thought I'd call in. Are you shocked?'

'Most pleasantly,' he replied, reaching for her hand and drawing her over the threshold. 'What new personality is this? Have you taken some magic potion?'

He led her into the living-room and caught up her other hand, holding them wide so as to look her up and down. Elizabeth felt a tiny blush creeping up her cheeks and hoped she had not appeared amenable too soon.

'I like your dress too. So charmingly unsuitable for a tutor.'

'I didn't come to see you as a tutor,' she said, smiling.

He dropped her right hand, but raised the other, idly fingering the black opal ring. 'Never tell me, my dear, that bad taste got the better of you and your beanpole fiancé!'

She could not control her hand from flinching. 'Why, whatever do you mean, Richard?'

His brows rose appreciatively at the use of his name.

'I mean, have you and Tim Bertram had a vulgar tiff? Is that the reason for this delightful surprise? If so, I can't say I'm flattered to be visited out of pique.'

She felt she had gained a foothold, and this gave her confidence. 'You know too much,' she agreed, with a little laugh. 'But please don't be offended. I came to see you because—well, because you're always so pleasant and—and friendly. I feel I could do with a pleasant friend for a while.'

'Well, that is some comfort,' he said lightly. 'We must see what progress can be made. There's such a dull ring about the word friendship.'

Elizabeth grew bolder. 'I had the impression that you were rather wanting to be friends for some time.'

He eyed her easily. 'Quite right, my dear. I knew it would only be a matter of time before I broke through that prim, frigid exterior of yours. Sit down while I fix some drinks. Then we can exchange troubles as a preliminary to getting to know each other better.'

Elizabeth curbed an impulse to retreat. She sank down on the couch which had been cleared of the debris that had littered it a day or so earlier, and retained her smile with an effort.

'Nothing to drink, thanks.'

'Oh, nonsense! Drink and trouble-telling go together. You can't possibly loosen your reserved tongue without some artificial aid.'

'I might say too much,' she said, in all truth.

'Then, I promise anything you say after your third drink will be forgotten.'

'Oh, very well, then,' she agreed, placing a rose-coloured cushion behind her dark head. She knew the colour suited her.

He opened a cabinet in one corner of the room and mixed drinks skilfully, whistling a tune under his breath. Then he set the glasses on a tray which he carried to the low coffee table near the couch.

'Comfortable?' he asked, switching on the lamp and going to the door to turn off the main light. He came back and stood looking down at her.

'Aren't you going to sit down?' asked Elizabeth nervously, picking up one of the glasses.

Craske sat down in silence, turning his own drink between his hands thoughtfully. 'Well, here's to our mutual troubles,' he said presently.

Elizabeth swallowed half her drink. She felt she needed it. 'What do you mean by mutual troubles?'

He gave her an impatient glance. 'Oh, my dear girl—don't try and pretend. I know you are only here at that inspector fellow's instigation.'

'You are quite mistaken. And if you think I wanted to bring him here the other day, you are also wrong.'

He laughed and touched her hand briefly. 'Yes, you did look as though you wished you were out of it,' he admitted. 'My deepest apologies.'

'You think I came here so as to—to spy on you for the police?' demanded Elizabeth, so affronted on this one count that she was able to forget her real reason was kin to it.

'I regret the unwarranted suspicion. Here, finish that up and let me get you another drink. Then I'll promise to stop looking for ulterior motives.'

Elizabeth followed his movements speculatively. Whether it was the brandy circulating through her system, or the fact that she had allayed his suspicions she did not know, but she was feeling pleased with herself. But she wished he had not set a record player in motion with dreamy music or reseated himself quite so close.

'Here, relax!' urged Craske pushing her gently against the cushion again. His hand lingered on her shoulder. 'I like my friends to be comfortable when they call.'

'Do you always entertain them like this?' she asked, a little breathlessly.

He leaned closer. 'The attractive female ones, anyway. And you're very feminine and more than attractive tonight, Elizabeth. Don't you think we have progressed enough from friendship?'

She lifted her glass hurriedly. 'You said we'd exchange troubles first. What are yours? Is there anything I can do to help?'

A fleeting expression of annoyance crossed his face, and he removed his hand. 'You are very kind,' he said dryly. 'Kind but unprogressive.'

'Perhaps you move too fast,' she suggested lightly. 'Perhaps that is why I have always been a little afraid of you.'

'Afraid of me!' Craske exclaimed, but Elizabeth could see he was flattered. He rested his arm along the back of the couch. 'Why, you absurd girl!'

She drooped her lashes. 'Well, after all, you have got rather a reputation. You must have been a sad trial to your wife.'

'My wife? Helena had nothing to complain about,' he said swiftly.

'She didn't mind your being pursued by other women?'

'She probably realized I couldn't stop 'em,' he replied, with a deprecatory laugh. 'But don't let's talk about the past. Let's talk about us.'

'And our mutual troubles?'

He sighed and took her hand. 'If you must. I can think of much pleasanter ways to pass the evening.'

'Is that why you have never remarried, Richard? Are you afraid that—' she stopped deliberately, pretending to search for words.

'What do you mean—afraid?' he asked roughly, his hand tightening on hers.

'Afraid that you'd never find anyone understanding enough to take Helena's place,' she finished, watching him from under her lashes. She knew she had scored a hit. His handsome face looked haggard suddenly, and all his easy confidence had dropped away. 'There's too much soda water in these drinks,' he said, rising abruptly. He was longer than necessary at the cabinet, and when he turned around he had regained his former nonchalance.

'Perhaps we'd be foolish, Elizabeth, to be ever anything more than agreeable sparring partners,' he suggested, looking down at her with smiling narrowed eyes. 'Just at the moment neither of us is feeling very happy. Let's do what we can to comfort each other— Oh, in a restrained sort of way, of course. You need not look so apprehensive.'

'I'm not apprehensive,' she retorted, taking her glass.

'Then you should be,' he said, sitting down. 'You're looking too damned attractive tonight. Why doesn't that fellow Bertram hurry up and marry you? Doesn't he realize what he's missing?'

'Why don't you hurry up and marry someone?' she rejoined, but this time the easy smiling mask remained unchanged. 'It's high time you had some capable wife to look after you. Why, this room was a shambles the other day and I daresay will be again soon—in spite of Thelma's good work.'

'That blasted wench! I haven't been able to find a thing since.'

Elizabeth seized the opening. 'What have you been looking for? Your raincoat?'

'My raincoat? Oh, no, that's somewhere around. Funny you should mention it. I thought I'd lost the thing, then quite suddenly it turned up in this very room.'

'That just goes to show you that you need a wife to keep check on your clothes alone.'

'What are you wishing on me—a female valet? Here, sit back and be comfortable again!' He pulled her gently info the crook of his arm and leaned his face against her hair. 'You don't mind, do you?' he murmured.

'I do rather,' she returned calmly. 'You seem to forget this.' She held up her engagement finger.

He covered it with his hand. 'Oh, damn that! Didn't we agree to comfort each other?'

'That was your suggestion, not mine.'

'Never mind whose suggestion—just think what an excellent idea it is. Will you come and see me again like this?'

'No, I don't think so,' she returned. 'There's no future in it for either of us.'

'First, you're concerned about the past and now it's the future. What about the present?'

The arm around Elizabeth's shoulder grew slowly rigid. 'I don't like women who throw themselves at my head and then try to back out,' he added softly. 'I'm not used to it.' Elizabeth's heart beat fast. 'So I understand,' she said trying to speak calmly. 'But you said yourself that we were better off as sparring partners. And then there is the small matter of my engagement.'

'Then why did you come here?' he inquired, in the same soft, menacing voice. There was an ominous pause.

'Perhaps if it were not for my engagement—' she began desperately.

'The matter of your engagement could possibly be rectified,' interrupted a new voice—a hard, angry voice.

Elizabeth looked across the room, aghast. Standing in the doorway was Timothy.

16

Elizabeth had never felt so ashamed and guilty before. She got up from Richard Craske's encircling arm and tried to speak coolly. 'What are you doing here, Timothy? Do you usually enter other people's houses without asking for admittance?'

Timothy's expression was that of a man unable to believe what his angry eyes saw. He answered in a rigidly controlled voice. 'I came here to take you back to your college, Elizabeth. As I was informed of my fiancée's presence in your house, Craske, I thought it was hardly necessary to do more than enter your open door.'

Craske, who had risen at leisure, said placatingly, 'Now, let's take things quietly. What about a drink?'

'No, thank you. Are you ready, Elizabeth?'

'No, I don't know that I am,' she replied, her own temper rising. Her nerves were already frayed from the events of the evening. 'You've interrupted a very pleasant tête-à-tête, Timothy. Who was it informed you I was here?'

'A message was conveyed to me from your Warden.'

'Mother Paul! But she—' she broke off, glancing quickly from one man to the other.

'I still think a drink would be a good way out of this embarrassing situation,' Craske remarked, with an uneasy laugh. 'What about it, Bertram? I'm sure you could use one.'

'The way I'd use a drink from you would be to throw it in your face,' snapped the other.

'Timothy!' exclaimed Elizabeth furiously.

'In that case I withdraw my offer,' said Craske, with a mocking bow. 'Don't be a fool, Bertram! Why shouldn't Elizabeth drop in for a friendly chat? She needs some sort of companionship occasionally, and if you're not prepared to give it to her—well, that's your lookout.'

'I'm not going to discuss our private affairs with you,' said Timothy, rather white around the mouth. 'Are you coming, Elizabeth?'

'Very well,' she replied, controlling herself with an effort. There was no sense in prolonging the unpleasant scene. 'Good night, Richard.'

Craske shrugged. 'Good night, my dear. Bad luck it had to end like this.'

'Perhaps it need not end,' said Elizabeth, mainly for Timothy's benefit.

His response was to take her arm urgently and to usher her from the house without more ado. Out in the street, he released his grip. 'And now, if you would just give me an explanation!'

She could have told him that she had visited Craske at Mother Paul's request, and with the greatest reluctance. But being emotionally distraught she instead tried to relieve her feelings. 'What makes you think I've got anything to explain?' she inquired dangerously. 'Remember I'm only engaged to you — not married.'

Timothy was in an equally combustible condition. 'Visiting that fellow's house at night! You must know the reputation he has. How many times have you been there? Has he tried to make love to you before this? Answer me, Elizabeth!'

'I'm not going to answer you,' she returned angrily. 'How dare you question where I go and what I do? What right have you — ?' She paused, and in a moment of overwrought rage tugged the ring from her left hand. 'Yes, I suppose you have some small right while I still wear this. Here, take it! Now, you've got no claim over me at all.'

Timothy clutched the ring automatically. 'Elizabeth! What are you doing? Here, put this back on at once. You're going to marry me.'

'When? When?' she demanded, her voice shaken between anger and tears. 'No, Timothy, it's been too long. I warned you. Right now I never want to see you again.' She tried to slip away, but he was after her at once, pinning her against the fence.

'I'm not going to accept that, Elizabeth. This is Craske's doing. He's flattered you, made you feel hardly done by.'

She beat against his chest with her closed fists. 'Let me go!'

'Well, I'm not going to try and imitate his way with every woman who crosses his path. All I know is I love you deeply, Elizabeth, and that I've always wanted you to be my wife.'

'Let me go!' she repeated furiously. 'How dare you make a scene like this on the street!'

'I make a scene!' Timothy's voice rose. 'Well, here's a fitting conclusion to it!'

Before Elizabeth knew what he was about, he had grabbed her roughly by the shoulders, bent his tall head and kissed her—the sort of kiss, she realized with deep mortification, she should not have liked.

'Does Craske do better than that?' Timothy demanded, releasing her.

With an angry sob, she broke away and ran through the gates of Brigid Moore Hall.

It did not take long for the students to notice the absence of their Humanities tutor's unusual engagement ring. Elizabeth reflected bitterly that the college could have been spared the hurly-burly of a Stunt Nite if she had known that her break with Timothy was going to cause so much whispered interest and curiosity. She considered that the Warden should be very grateful to her for providing another diversion. But she had not yet seen Mother Paul, and as the morning progressed, she had a strong impression that the nun was deliberately avoiding her.

Preparation for Stunt Nite was going on in the lecture hall of the Cottage. A temporary stage was being noisily erected, the piano had been wheeled across from the recreation room and the students, in their free periods, were busy turning the hall into a festive scene with coloured streamers and bright posters. The tutors' sitting-room had been taken over as a dressing-room, and Miss Dove was in the process of removing her choicer objets d'art to safety.

'Remember that Meissen figurine someone knocked over last year?' she remarked to Elizabeth, in between sorties from the sitting-room to her bedroom. 'Youngsters today seem to have little regard for the property of others.'

The telephone rang and Miss Dove, carefully putting down the ormolu clock she had been carrying like a fragile baby, went to answer it.

Her voice changed, becoming brighter and brisker. She glanced over her shoulder at Elizabeth, who took it for a hint and made to leave the room.

But Miss Dove stopped her by holding out the receiver. 'For you—Professor Craske!' She gave Elizabeth one of her sidelong glances and then went swiftly out of the room.

'Elizabeth?' asked Richard Craske's voice caressingly. 'Are you alone?'

'Yes! What do you want?'

'Is it true you've broken your engagement?'

'Yes, it's true.'

'Because of last night?'

'That topped an accumulation.'

There was silence over the line. 'Is that all you wanted to know?' asked the girl, stonily.

'Will you have lunch with me today?'

'No! At least—yes, all right. Thank you.' There was no reason why she should not lunch with Craske.

'Fine! The Union at twelve-thirty then?'

Timothy always lunched there when he was working in the Anthropological museum. 'I'll be there,' she said and rang off. She turned and found Miss Dove standing in the doorway.

'I came back for the cushions,' said the Science tutor in a toneless voice.

'Is there anything else you want moved?'

'No, that will be all. Miss Drew—!'

'Yes, what is it?'

'I —I'm sorry to hear about your change of—of marriage plans. You and Dr Bertram seemed so ideally suited.'

'I appreciate your concern,' replied Elizabeth coldly, 'but I would be even more appreciative if you would not refer to the matter.'

A flush spread over the other's smooth, sallow skin. 'I—I beg your pardon,' she muttered stiffly. She backed away and nearly fell against the Warden, who had suddenly appeared in the doorway. 'Excuse me. Reverend Mother.'

'Accidents will happen,' rejoined the nun cheerfully. She watched her go and then wafted into the room, shutting the door carefully behind her. 'I was looking for you, Elizabeth.'

'And I was rather wanting to see you,' replied the girl, a trifle grimly.

'Were you, dear? About the Whipples, I suppose. I've just had a telephone call from the Dean. He wants to know what I think of his position. Quite at cross-purposes we were until he told me to ask you for an explanation. What is it all about, Elizabeth?'

Far more immersed in her own troubles, the girl had difficulty in dragging herself back to the beginning of the disastrous night. She told the nun of her meeting with the Dean and the story of his entanglement with Helena Craske.

The Warden listened intently. 'What an odd sort of creature Mrs Craske must have been,' she observed mildly. 'Rather silly too, I should say. A typical murder victim.'

'Mother Paul, you don't think that Professor Whipple—?'

'Nothing surprises me when it comes to the complex emotions people in the world seem to suffer from,' said the nun frankly. 'I can't understand how anyone can endure it. You say that when Maureen saw Professor Whipple she ran away?'

'That is what he told me.'

'How odd!' said the nun softly. After a pause she asked, 'Mrs Whipple—what sort of person is she?'

Elizabeth described her. 'She's fiercely loyal and protective towards the Dean,' she added.

'And we only have her word for it that she was far from the University that day?'

'She probably could supply an alibi if need be,' said Elizabeth. 'But I don't think either of them realizes that Mr Savage's inquiries concern murder.'

'And Mrs Whipple has red hair?'

Elizabeth smiled. 'Dyed, I'm afraid.'

There was another pause. 'How odd!' repeated the Warden, in a gentle absent way. Then she became more alert. 'Now, tell me about Professor Craske's raincoat.'

The smile faded from Elizabeth's face. 'He has no idea how it was returned,' she said shortly.

'You're certain he was speaking the truth?'

'Quite certain.'

'I see,' said the nun thoughtfully. She drew out the notebook and placed her spectacles on her nose. 'No, it would probably not occur to him.' She made a note in her book then slipped it into the capacious slip pocket of her habit.

'Well, dear, is that all you have to report?' she asked in a bright voice.

'Not quite,' replied Elizabeth tersely. 'Did you know I am no longer engaged?'

'Yes, I heard,' said the Warden, avoiding her gaze. 'So upsetting for you, but things will work out all right in the end, I'm sure.'

'Mother Paul,' said Elizabeth distinctly, watching her. 'Last night I was placed in an acutely embarrassing and painful position.'

'Oh dear, was it that bad?' murmured the nun, looking contrite.

Elizabeth took a deep breath. 'Mother Paul, did you deliberately conspire to have Timothy appear in Richard Craske's house? Was that your idea of giving him a jolt?'

The Warden bowed her head. 'I always understood a little jealousy worked wonders.'

'Oh, yes, there's nothing like jealousy,' said Elizabeth bitterly. 'Timothy reacted so magnificently that I told him I never want to see him again.'

'And what about Professor Craske?' asked the nun, in a small voice. But she was watching the girl intently.

'Oh, he knows I've broken with Tim. He wants me to lunch with him at the Union today.'

'Are you going to?'

'Yes, I am,' said Elizabeth defiantly. 'And I hope Timothy sees me. Anyway, someone will be certain to tell him. Matters like this are grist to the University gossips' mill.'

'Splendid!' said the Warden, beaming on her. 'Nothing could be better. And poor Dr Bertram will never suspect how much you regret the drastic move of breaking your engagement.'

'Never?' echoed Elizabeth, suddenly stricken. 'But he must know. I don't want to make him jealous any more than I want to encourage Richard Craske. I'm not made for these sort of games.'

'Of course not, dear,' said the nun soothingly. 'Much too nice a character. But there are times, so I have been told, when women have to pretend a little. So you will promise to keep on as you have begun, won't you, Elizabeth?'

There was a note of urgency in her voice, which should have put the girl on her guard. But Elizabeth was thinking remorsefully of

Timothy and wondering how long it would take him to see through the pretence. 'I suppose there's nothing else I can do for the moment,' she agreed drearily.

Unseen by her, the Warden nodded to herself in a satisfied manner.

That Fiona Searle was up to something became more obvious to those who knew her mercurial temperament. Excitement over Stunt Nite was running high among the students, but Fiona's restlessness and vivacity stood out. Very soon, the circle of those in the know widened, until, at the last moment, a hint of what Fiona was about reached Elizabeth's ears.

She had been absent from the college most of what to her had been a thoroughly miserable day. She had had no sight or word of Timothy, and she soon regretted her rashness in being seen with Richard Craske. There had been a tutors' meeting in Baillieu in the late afternoon, at which Elizabeth had sensed that already their names were being coupled.

She got back to the Cottage only in time to change for the students' performance. Their chatter and excited giggles reached her from the sitting-room where they were getting ready. Just as well someone's happy, thought Elizabeth with a shrug. She closed her bedroom door on the results of a lightning change and went down the passage.

Then, as she was passing the sitting-room door. She overheard one of the students saying doubtfully, 'Well, I still think it's rather a mean trick. Judith is likely to take it badly.'

Elizabeth paused as Fiona's voice came back. 'Oh, rubbish! She ought to be thrilled to catch a glimpse of the long-lost sister. Anyway, it's going to be the highlight of the night, so stop pulling a long face.'

Elizabeth's own face set into exasperated lines. She kicked open the door and stood on the threshold, surveying them. 'All right, Fiona! What mischief are you brewing now?'

Fiona, devastatingly attractive in bright theatrical makeup and a shimmering knee-length frock, lounged across the room nonchalantly. 'No mischief, Liz,' she replied cheekily, swinging her long jade beads around one forefinger.

'I don't believe you,' said Elizabeth, with a snap. 'What's going to be the highlight of the night?'

'Wait and see!'

There was a silence in the crowded room. Then one of the girls said nervously, 'You'd better tell Miss Drew, Fiona.'

'Oh, you!' said Fiona sulkily. 'Of all the weak-kneed—! The highlight is going to be a little treat for Judith Mornane—and the Warden too. Haven't we heard enough about Maureen Mornane these last few days? Okay! Now we are going to see her.'

'What do you mean?'

'Peter Baynes has some film shots of last year's Orientation. Maureen is in them and he is going to show them tonight.'

Elizabeth looked at her. 'Are your intentions cruel or kind, Fiona?'

The girl grinned and performed an impudent Charleston step. 'Say a mixture of both. What are you going to do about it?'

Elizabeth hesitated. 'I'll have to tell the Warden. It will be up to her to decide whether the film will be shown.' Monica, who was acting as stage manager, loped up behind Elizabeth. 'I say, you girls! Everyone's waiting, so look slippy! Who's on first? Aren't you coming to Stunt Nite, Miss Drew? The Warden's been asking for you.'

'Yes, I'm coming, Monica.' Elizabeth stood aside to let the performers pass first. Then she followed and stood at the back of the lecture hall until the first item, a song and dance chorus featuring sly, topical lyrics set, with blithe disregard for copyright, to one of the latest hit tunes, was over.

There was an empty seat in the second row just behind the nuns, who were applauding with the prodigal enthusiasm of children. Elizabeth slid into it and whispered, 'Mother Paul!'

The Warden turned her head. 'Oh, there you are, Elizabeth!' Then she saw the girl's grave face. 'What is it, child?'

'That boy Baynes from Manning College! Fiona has asked him over to show films of last year's Orientation week. He has some shots of Maureen Mornane.'

The Warden's eyes widened and her lips parted in a silent circle. For a moment she seemed bereft of speech, and could only stare at Elizabeth as though she found it hard to take in what the girl had said.

'Mother Paul, do you think it wise for these films to be shown? Fiona's being malicious, I'm afraid. She's been deliberately softening Judith up for this.'

The nun seemed to rouse herself. 'Yes, yes, of course! Naughty Fiona. And Judith has no idea?'

Elizabeth glanced over her shoulder. Judith was sitting a row or two back. She saw the tutor's glance and smiled back at her happily.

'No, Judith doesn't know.'

The Warden's attention was on the stage where two Asian students, clad in colourful costumes, were beginning one of their national dances. She whispered rapidly, 'Go over to the main house and ring Inspector Savage. Tell him to come at once—that it is very, very important.'

'You mean you want him to see the films?'

The nun's eyes gleamed. 'I want him to see Judith as well as the films. Ask her to come and sit where you are now. Go quickly, Elizabeth!'

Elizabeth half rose in her seat, caught Judith's eye again and beckoned her with a reassuring smile. Looking rather puzzled, Judith made her way along the row of freshettes with whom she had been sitting.

'The Warden wants you to sit near her,' explained Elizabeth in a whisper, as they met in the aisle. 'I'll be back presently.' She waited only to see Judith safely seated behind the Warden, and then left the lecture hall as unobtrusively as possible.

But she was barely out of the Cottage when a voice called after her. 'Miss Drew!'

Elizabeth glanced over her shoulder. Miss Dove was standing silhouetted in the lighted front door. There was a sharp, insistent note in the Science tutor's voice as she asked. 'Where are you going? Why are you leaving the concert?'

'Over to the main house. The Warden wants me to do an errand for her.'

Miss Dove closed the door behind her and approached through the darkened garden. 'I don't believe you!' she said harshly. 'You planned to slip away.'

Elizabeth knew what she was thinking. 'Mother Paul asked me to ring Inspector Savage. Peter Baynes is bringing some films she considers he should see.'

Miss Dove's breathing was audible. 'I still don't believe you. If the Warden wanted that policeman at the Stunt Nite, she would have asked him earlier.'

Elizabeth quelled a spurt of anger. She was coming close to disliking Miss Dove heartily. 'We only learned of the existence of these films a short time ago. The important part is that they include shots of Maureen Mornane.'

There was a pause. Then Miss Dove exclaimed in a shaking voice, 'Maureen Mornane! I wish I'd never heard that name.'

Turning, she hurried away into the darkness.

The main house was quiet and empty as Elizabeth let herself in. She pressed down the main switches in both the hall and the students' recreation room and went to the telephone.

She got through to Savage's office almost immediately and requested that an urgent message be conveyed to come at once to Brigid Moore Hall. 'Tell him that it is important and that I will wait for him at the main house,' she said, before replacing the receiver. She went back into the hall and paced restlessly to and fro. The strange effect that the news of Peter Baynes's film had had on the usually imperturbable Warden puzzled her. But Mother Paul evidently expected Savage would regard the urgent call worth complying with.

I wish he and Mother Paul could come to some decision and finish this ghastly business, thought Elizabeth. She found herself making comparisons between the unsettled affairs at Brigid Moore and her own uprooted life, and reached one of the illogical feminine conclusions that until the one was solved the other would never be.

Presently the doorbell rang shrilly through the silent house, making Elizabeth jump nervously. She went forward quickly and opened the door, prepared to see Inspector Savage. Instead a shorter, slighter figure, leaning heavily against the jamb, met her startled gaze. It was Peter Baynes.

He just managed to step over the threshold before he slumped to the floor.

17

'What on earth's the matter with you?' demanded Elizabeth, shock causing her to speak sharply.

The boy seemed incapable of speech. He was breathing heavily and his face was buried in the hood of his duffle coat.

Elizabeth knelt beside him. 'Here, sit up! Are you ill or something? They're expecting you at the Cottage. Why did you come here?'

'Help me, will you?' Peter said, in a blurred voice.

'Why, you're hurt!' exclaimed Elizabeth, catching sight of a trickle of blood on his cheek. 'Did a car knock you down coming across Cemetery Road?'

He shook his head dumbly. His eyes were closed and he looked very pale.

Elizabeth surveyed him with critical anxiety. 'Stay quiet for a moment. I'll get some water to clean you up. You can't be seen like that.' She hurried away to the downstairs cloakroom, swiftly wrung out a towel with cold water and picked up another.

Peter Baynes was still sitting propped against the wall, but he seemed more alert and was feeling the side of his head gingerly. Elizabeth cleaned his face of blood and dust with a briskness that made him wince.

'Sorry! Here, hold this wet towel against the lump on your head.' She made it into a pad and gave it to him. Then she sat back on her heels. 'Where's your equipment? I thought you were coming over to show films.'

'Someone took them,' replied the boy. 'I can't remember too clearly, but someone hit me on the head. When I woke up both my projector and the bag I carry spools in were gone.'

'Whose idea of a joke—?' began Elizabeth indignantly. The film shots of Maureen Mornane, which had caused Mother Paul such a strange excitement! 'You're sure they're gone?' she asked foolishly.

Peter Baynes nodded painfully. 'And it wasn't a joke, I can tell you.'

'Who was it hit you?' demanded Elizabeth, although she knew it was a futile question.

'I haven't a clue. I say, do you mind leaving the questions? My head is nearly splitting.' He closed his eyes again and gave himself up to his agony.

Elizabeth surveyed him helplessly. Then, as the doorbell rang again, she jumped up, saying, 'I'm afraid you're going to have to forget your head. That should be Inspector Savage.'

Peter's eyes flashed wide. 'The detective type? Why's he coming here? I don't want to see him.'

'Well, someone's got to know about this attack of yours.'

Savage stepped into the hall briskly. 'Your message reached me at Professor Whipple's house. What is the trouble, Miss Drew?' His gaze fell on Peter Baynes. 'Someone been hurt?'

'No, I'm just sitting here for the fun of it,' muttered the boy hostilely, struggling to rise.

'You're the young man I interviewed at Manning College, aren't you?' asked Savage. 'Here, let me help you.'

'We'd better go into the parlour,' said Elizabeth, in a worried voice and led the way. 'The supper girls will be over from the Cottage soon. I suppose you're wondering what all this is about, Inspector. The students are having a Stunt Nite. The Warden asked me to call you urgently in order that you could see some films Peter was going to show. There were some shots of Maureen Mornane amongst them.'

'How did you know that?' asked the boy, sinking into a chair and dropping his head in his hands. 'Fiona said she wasn't going to tell anyone.'

'Where are these films?' asked Savage.

The boy let out a bitter crack of laughter. 'That's what I'd like to know. Someone bushwhacked me on the way over.'

Savage looked at Elizabeth with raised brows. 'Does Mother Paul know about this?'

'Not yet. I was waiting here for you when Peter arrived in this condition.' She went to the open parlour door, and called to a couple of girls who had come back to see to the supper. 'Would one of you please go over to the Cottage and tell the Warden she is wanted urgently!'

'What made you come here, Mr Baynes, after you had been—er—bushwhacked? Wouldn't it have been more reasonable to go back to your own college?'

'I didn't think of it,' replied Peter, submitting with a bad grace to having the lump on his head examined by the detective. 'I thought I'd better tell Fiona about the films.'

Savage drew Elizabeth aside. 'Well, he certainly couldn't have inflicted a lump like that on himself.'

'What does it all mean?' asked the girl. 'We didn't know about the films until a short time ago. Mother Paul seemed quite excited about them.'

'With justification evidently. Whatever that film contained concerning Maureen Mornane was too dangerous to be shown. You say no one knew about its existence?' Elizabeth glanced across at the Manning undergraduate. 'Well, he did, of course—and I suppose some of his friends at Manning. Quite a few of the students here knew that Fiona Searle was planning it as an unpleasant surprise for Judith. There has been a bit of friction the last few days.'

'Quite a number of persons knew, then,' said Savage. 'Can you account for everyone at Brigid Moore at the concert?'

Elizabeth hesitated. 'The students giving items should have been either in the Cottage sitting-room or on the stage. Miss Dove left when the Warden sent me over here.'

'You mean she came with you? She knew about the films?'

'I told her about them,' Elizabeth admitted grudgingly. 'But she didn't come with me. I—I don't know where she was going.'

'I see,' said Savage, and was silent.

Elizabeth ventured a question. 'You were with Professor Whipple just now. Did he tell you about—about knowing Helena Craske?'

'Yes, he asked me to come and see him. You and Mother Paul know his story?'

Elizabeth nodded. 'When you were there, was—was Mrs Whipple in the room?'

Savage looked at her. 'The Dean said she was at home. I heard occasional movements.'

They both turned at the sound of a familiar rustle of serge skirts and wooden rosary beads. The Warden entered the room swiftly. She was followed by Judith who wore an anxious, puzzled expression and Fiona, still dressed in her 'twenties costume with her stage make-up on.

'Peter!' exclaimed Fiona, darting forward. 'Oh, Peter—what's happened? This is all my fault.'

The boy gave a shaky laugh and tried to get up. 'Unless it was you who hit me, it is hardly your fault, Fiona. My films and projector have been stolen too.'

She pressed him back into his chair. 'Then it is my fault. I should have told the Warden about them at once. I was trying to be clever. There's someone who doesn't want Maureen Mornane found. Heather knew something and look what happened!' She shook his shoulder. 'Peter, you've got to tell the police everything! You'll be murdered too, if you're not careful.'

'Oh, now, Fiona,' Peter protested feebly, glancing at the others.

Fiona flung back her head and faced Savage. 'That's what it is, isn't it? Murder! Judith has been the only game one to come out in the open and say so. Well, I'm game now, too. Murder! Murder!' she said, her voice rising hysterically.

'Stop it, Fiona!' commanded Elizabeth.

'I won't stop,' cried Fiona, with short heaving breaths. 'There's been enough hush-hush business. How I hate it—hate everyone—!'

The Warden swept forward and gave her a smart slap across one brightly rouged cheek. After a wide, astonished glance, Fiona burst into tears.

'I'm so sorry, dear,' said Mother Paul apologetically, as the girl sank her head on Judith Mornane's shoulder. Then she said to Peter Baynes, 'Fiona's suggestion was admirable. You must tell us everything you know. Believe me, Inspector Savage is an excellent listener—so open-minded.'

Savage's lips twitched momentarily. 'All right now, Peter! Where do you fit into all this?'

'All what?' asked the boy guardedly. 'I told you I hardly knew either the Mornane girl or Heather Markham.'

'But you did know Helena Craske,' prompted the Warden gently.

'Yes, I knew Mrs Craske,' said the boy unhappily. 'But what—what has she to do—?'

Savage interrupted him. 'Now look, Peter! We're going to examine the position with surface-value facts for the moment. Those facts are Mrs Craske's accidental death from drowning, Maureen Mornane's disappearance, and Heather Markham's suicide. What truths lie behind those facts are not your concern if you can explain your position satisfactorily. Do you follow me?'

'I—I think so.'

'Then tell me of your friendship with the late Mrs Craske.'

'There's—there's not much to tell. I knew her fairly well for a while. She—she used to like my coming to see her. I sometimes wrote poetry and stuff which I read to her. I thought she was only being encouraging and kind—that she was only interested in—' Peter broke off and looked at Savage imploringly. 'You know what I mean. Do I have to go on?'

'No, you don't have to, Peter,' he said kindly. 'I've heard similar stories about Mrs Craske.'

The boy gave him a grateful glance. 'When Helena—died, and they said it was an accident, I was terribly relieved. You see—she had threatened to commit suicide because—well, because I didn't want to have anything more to do with her. You do believe me, don't you?' he added anxiously, as Savage was silent.

But the inspector was too experienced to commit himself. Instead he asked, 'Had you taken some definite stand with Mrs Craske? Did you ever tell her, for example, that you would not see her again?'

The boy licked his lips. 'I tried to—several times. Then she would talk about suicide and—and I felt I had to keep on seeing her.'

'Then right up to her death you still had not severed relations?'

'No! I dared not after what she had threatened to do.'

'Then if Mrs Craske did commit suicide, she certainly wouldn't have done so on your account.'

Peter stared at him, the haggard expression slowly leaving his face. 'Why no—no, she couldn't have, could she? I didn't think of it like that.'

'On the other hand,' said Savage, a hard note in his voice. 'You were very much relieved when you heard she was dead. You had badly wanted to be free of her.'

'What do you mean?'

'I was wondering just what you would have done if Mrs Craske had not had that accident in her bath,' said Savage sternly.

'Nothing! I wouldn't have done anything. I've told you everything I can. Why do you keep on badgering me—hinting at something ghastly?'

'Yes, how dare you!' exclaimed Fiona. 'Why don't you do something about the person who attacked Peter instead of all this mudraking? Helena Craske has been dead for ages. And what about Maureen Mornane? What did Heather Markham have to do with her disappearance—that is, if she did disappear? Why don't you find out what happened to Maureen?'

'Hush, child!' said Mother Paul.

'Well, it's because of Maureen that Peter was attacked tonight.' Fiona turned to Judith. 'Your sister! Film shots with your sister in them. Why did someone not want them shown?'

'I can't understand it,' said Peter, in a puzzled voice. 'They were just ordinary shots. Maureen wasn't in them for any length of time either.'

'Judith, have you any idea?' Fiona asked, but the other girl shook her head.

'Stand still, Judith!' said the Warden suddenly. 'Fiona, I want you to have a good look at this girl. Cast your mind back a year. Try and remember yourself as you were then. Look closely at her.'

'I'm looking,' said Fiona, in a bewildered voice. 'What do you want me to see?'

'I want you to see—Maureen Mornane,' said the nun softly. 'Could not this girl be the one you knew last year?'

Judith let out a smothered cry. 'Mother Paul, what are you—?'

'Maureen Mornane!' said Fiona, in a whisper. Her eyes were wide and intent.

'No, I'm Judith! I'm Judith!'

'Could she be Maureen, Fiona?'

Elizabeth's heart beat fast. She glanced at Savage, who was watching the scene closely.

Then Peter Baynes broke the tension. 'This is not the girl in my film,' he said. 'Nothing like her, in fact. Of course the red hair not showing up makes a considerable difference.'

'Well, Fiona? What do you say?'

Fiona shook her head. 'I can't remember clearly what Maureen looked like, but I'm sure she was taller than Judith here. You are Judith, aren't you?' she added, with an uncertain laugh.

Judith's lips were trembling. 'Of course I am. Mother Paul, why did you—?'

'Just a little experiment, dear. You know, but for what Peter said I think I could almost have persuaded everyone you were Maureen.' She gave an apologetic laugh. 'But I am wasting Mr Savage's time. He must be wondering what I am about.'

'Yes, I am,' said the inspector bluntly.

'Please go on, Mr Savage. I promise not to interrupt again.'

'I have no further questions to ask,' he said, watching her closely. 'It seems we have lost a very important clue to Maureen's whereabouts. Unfortunate, but there is nothing we can do about it.'

'Sometimes misfortunes can be blessings in disguise,' said the Warden. She did not seem at all cast down, a fact that was puzzling Savage, so Elizabeth considered. She herself was completely at a loss and felt a certain sympathy for Peter when he exclaimed. 'But what about the person who slugged me! And my film outfit? It's worth far more to me than any clue.'

'Then I suggest you have another look for it,' said Savage. 'It is certain to have been abandoned somewhere close to where you were struck down.'

'Judith and I will go with you,' offered Fiona eagerly. 'No, you must stay in the college, dear,' the Warden corrected gently. 'I want you both to carry on with Stunt Nite as though nothing has happened.'

Fiona looked rebellious for a moment. Then Judith said shyly, 'Come on, Fiona! You always make things more fun for everyone.'

'Oh, all right,' said the other. She turned back to Peter for a moment. 'Well—see you!' she said uncertainly.

When the students had gone, the Warden said, 'You had better stay in the parlour until the girls are all at supper, Peter. Miss Drew will tell you when to leave. Would you care to step into my office for a few minutes, Mr Savage?'

'Certainly!' he replied promptly, and followed her from the room.

Elizabeth tried not to feel resentful at being left out. She turned and saw the boy's eyes on her.

'What's it all about, Miss Drew?' he asked anxiously. 'Fiona said you knew.'

'Only up to a point.'

'It's — it's pretty grim, isn't it?'

'Yes, pretty grim. That sounds like the girls now.' She waited with the parlour door open a crack until the students, laughing and chattering, filed through the hall on their way to the dining-room. 'We'd better give them five minutes to settle down.'

Presently she led him out by the front door. Then she turned and stared undecidedly at the closed door of the Warden's office.

It opened abruptly and Inspector Savage came out. His face was set in a grim expression. He saw Elizabeth and hesitated, as though there was something he could have said to her. Instead he spoke over his shoulder to the nun standing in the doorway of the office, 'You'll hear from me in a day or so, Mother Paul. I only hope you are right.'

With a brief nod to Elizabeth, he went swiftly out of the house.

Elizabeth looked at the nun, waiting for her to explain what she and Savage had been discussing behind the closed door. But all the Warden said was, 'Shall we join the girls for supper now, Elizabeth?'

18

A vague impression that the Warden no longer relied upon her persisted with Elizabeth. But there was something unapproachable about the nun which prevented the girl making any overture. She felt rather indignant at the sudden abandonment—indignant and more than a little hurt. She now had neither Timothy nor Mother Paul, and in consequence fell back on Richard Craske's spurious attentions less dubiously. Loneliness made her uncaring and she allowed herself to be seen in his company without any attempt at discretion. Rumours coupling their names would amuse rather than irk Craske. But when the time came for them to part, somehow he would let it be known that it was he who had given the Brigid Moore tutor her *congé*. It had happened before with other female members of the University personnel.

The evening following Stunt Nite, he took Elizabeth to dinner at a little continental restaurant in the city. She was feeling tired and dull and knew he was probably finding her boring, but she did not care. She had only accepted his invitation so as to get away from Brigid Moore for a while.

When coffee was served to them, he suddenly reached across for her hand. She gave an audible sigh, but allowed her hand to lie inertly in his clasp.

'You don't really like me, do you, Elizabeth?' he said softly.

She glanced up startled. 'Of course I like you,' she protested, automatically. 'I wouldn't be having dinner with you unless I liked you.'

An unpleasant look came into his eyes. 'Wouldn't you?'

'I know I haven't been very entertaining company,' she admitted. 'I'm a little tired.'

'When are you making it up with Bertram?' he asked, still watching her.

'That is my business,' she replied coldly.

'My business too. I wouldn't like to think I am being played off against an erstwhile fiancé.'

'What a suspicious person you are!' she said, smiling with an effort. 'You are always crediting me with some ulterior motive. First of all I was spying for Inspector Savage and now I'm dining with you to—to make Timothy jealous.'

The mean expression faded as he laughed. 'I don't usually bother about the ulterior motives of women. They are never worth my attention.'

'Then I should feel flattered,' replied the girl smoothly.

'No woman is above flattery,' he agreed, and she could see that his suspicions were lulled. But his next question put her instantly on guard. 'Tell me,' he asked casually. 'Has that policeman of yours finished his snooping? I haven't seen him about for a while.'

'He is coming back to see the Warden in a day or so.'

'What exactly was he after? He seems to have put the wind up various people.'

'But not you?' she asked bluntly.

'Why should I be worried? Oh, you mean that unwarranted question he put regarding Helena. I can't think what was behind it.' But his manner was just a shade too off hand.

He is hiding something, thought Elizabeth. He always has been hiding something. Suddenly she felt an angry curiosity to find out what it was he was frightened about.

'I can tell you,' she heard herself saying, almost without volition.

The pinched expression distorted his handsome face again. He leaned across the table. 'Tell me!' he said roughly.

Already she regretted her impulse. 'I'll tell you only on one condition,' she whispered. 'That morning over a year ago, when your—your wife died—where were you? What were you doing?'

His reply came promptly. 'I was lecturing from eight-thirty onwards in the Science building. Then I was with Professor Whipple in his study.'

Elizabeth searched his face. 'You didn't go home at all? You were with someone all that morning?'

'I can prove it.'

'Then you couldn't have—couldn't—'

'Go on,' he urged harshly.

Elizabeth's eyes were on his changed face. 'You—you couldn't have had anything to do with her—her death,' she faltered.

'Oh, you little fool!' he exclaimed. 'Speak up, can't you? What does Savage really think?'

Elizabeth's mouth felt dry. 'He thinks Helena might have been—murdered. And that Maureen Mornane was a witness.'

'Then she must be dead too,' he said flatly. 'Well? And what about that other student who hanged herself? What does he think really happened?'

'Heather knew something. The suicide was faked.'

For a moment Craske said nothing. His face was haggard and he slowly pressed one clenched fist on the table. Then he looked at Elizabeth. 'So that's it! And Savage thinks I had something to do with the killings. No wonder he's lying low. He can't prove a thing, can he?' When the girl did not reply, he repeated, 'Can he prove any part of these nonsensical assertions?'

'You're frightened!' she accused him defiantly. 'You've been frightened for a long time now. I think you guessed part of what happened. Somehow you knew about Helena.'

He gave her a terrible look. 'You say that to Savage or anyone else and I'll—' He got up abruptly and made a sign to a waiter. 'We're going now,' he told Elizabeth.

'I'll go home by myself,' she said, suddenly frightened herself.

'No, you're coming with me,' he said smoothly. 'I want to hear more.'

'I haven't finished my coffee. Can't we stay here and talk?'

But Craske had already dropped a couple of notes on the bill. He took Elizabeth's arm and pulled her up.

'What about your change?' she asked. But he led her away, his hand firmly under her elbow.

Outside they were caught up in a crowd. It was the first night of a Ray Lawler play at the adjoining theatre. Elizabeth felt her fears lighten. She would make a sudden break and slip away from Craske.

'My car is in the parking lot around the corner,' said Craske's mocking voice in her ear. 'I regret making you walk. But I do so enjoy your company, my dear.'

She pretended to stumble and, wrenching herself free, pushed sideways through the crowd. She was wedged in a mass of bodies and struck out blindly, regardless of the protesting moon faces turning her way. She caught a glistening glimpse of cars drawing up to unload more bodies and thrust her way towards the kerb. She would get across the street and find a taxi somewhere to take her back to Brigid Moore before Craske found her.

The crowd had overflowed the pavement and the theatre's commissionaire was shepherding them back. Elizabeth avoided his pontifical arm. She remembered feeling the edge of the kerb under her feet, and seeing a car's hood approaching over the swaying heads about her. Then, with a terrifying clarity, it happened. Not the nudging or jostling of an impatient crowd, but a well-defined push. Two hands thrust at her back.

She lost balance and the next moment was sprawling on the roadway with the headlights of the car looming over her. There was a screech of brakes and a roar from the crowd. Winded by fright and the heavy fall, Elizabeth lay still. The moon faces gathered around and there were sharp exclamations of alarm.

'Take it easy, Miss!' It was the theatre's commissionaire. 'Keep back, everyone. Give the young lady air.'

'Help me up,' begged Elizabeth. She felt bruised all over. The man put an arm under her and raised her up. A policeman appeared on the scene and the driver of the car which had nearly struck her.

'It's all right,' said the girl, with an effort. 'I slipped on the kerb. If you could just get me a taxi—?'

'Miss Drew! I could hardly believe my eyes. Are you hurt?' Miss Dove's voice and face registered hastily.

'Just shaken, I'd say,' said the policeman dispassionately. 'You are a friend of this lady's? You'd better get her home.'

'My cab is free,' offered the driver, magnanimous from relief.

'Lean on me,' Miss Dove told Elizabeth as she helped her into the taxi. 'What in the world happened?'

'I was with Richard—Professor Craske,' replied Elizabeth vaguely, looking back into the crowd. 'Did you see him?'

'Not anywhere near you. You must have become separated by the crowd. I was waiting for Ruby Whipple when I saw you fall. We have tickets for the Ray Lawler play.'

'Please don't miss the first act for my sake,' said Elizabeth. 'I'm quite all right now. Mrs Whipple will be wondering where you are.'

'Well, if you're sure—' Miss Dove said dubiously. 'Driver, will you stop a minute?'

The taxi glided into the kerb and Miss Dove put a hand on the door. 'You still haven't told me what happened.'

Elizabeth lips twisted. 'Didn't you see?' she asked. 'Someone pushed me.'

Miss Dove hesitated. Then she opened the door quickly. 'You're imagining things,' she muttered. 'You want to watch what you say— and in future look before you leap.' She stepped out and slammed the door after her.

Elizabeth gave the driver instructions and then closed her eyes wearily. Mrs Whipple or Miss Dove? she thought. It couldn't have been Richard Craske. And yet—he must have known about the accident. Things like that spread through a crowd like wildfire.

The following day was overcast and oppressive. Elizabeth felt tired and far from well as she tried to pursue her normal duties. The misadventure of the night before continually weighed on her, but she kept vacillating over the details. Perhaps it had been a genuine accident which her flight from Craske had distorted into something else. Then she would remember the hands jabbing at the small of her back and realize, with a stab of fear, that an attempt had been made on her life.

By afternoon she could no longer stand the strain of her indecision. Whether or not the Warden trusted her, the welfare and safety of the staff was her concern.

Mother Paul was still behaving elusively, but Elizabeth seized the opportunity at tea time when the nun was passing round the afternoon mail to ask for an interview.

'Very well!' agreed the Warden, but she gave the impression of reluctance. 'I'll be in my office in a few moments.'

'It's very important,' Elizabeth said quietly, aware of Miss Dove close at hand. The Science tutor's attention did not seem wholly on the letter she was reading as she sipped from a cup of tea.

Elizabeth took her own tea to the other side of the dining-room and opened the envelope Mother Paul had put into her hand. It bore the crest of Manning College and she presumed its typewritten contents to be a circular concerning tutors' lectures.

In the original concept of genetics—ran a solitary line at the top of the page. Puzzled, Elizabeth turned the sheet. Then her heart gave a great leap as she saw it was a letter from Timothy. He had evidently used a sheet of paper discarded from the Moran lecture he was typing.

Her mouth curved tenderly as she read: *Elizabeth, darling! Please let me see you. I'll be in the Considine museum tonight at ten. Don't fail me. All my love, Timothy.*

She read the note through twice, feeling happier than she had for days, then slipped it into her pocket and left the room.

Mother Paul was busy with her own letters. She glanced up briefly. 'Ah, Elizabeth! Come in, dear. What is the trouble?'

Elizabeth shut the door carefully. 'I want to know why anyone should try to kill me,' she said quietly.

Mother Paul's head jerked up. She looked over her spectacles with wide eyes. 'Kill you, child?' she repeated incredulously. 'Surely you are imagining things.'

'Sometimes I tell myself that,' the girl agreed, but her voice shook. 'I want to know what you think. It happened last night after I—I had dined with Professor Craske in town. There was a big crowd when we came out of the restaurant. Professor Craske and I became—separated. Not long afterwards I felt a push and fell on the roadway in front of a car.'

'Elizabeth!' exclaimed the nun swiftly.

'I wasn't hurt—only bruised, and—and frightened. Miss Dove got me a taxi. She was waiting for Mrs Whipple. They were going to the theatre together. So you see, Mother Paul, there were three persons from the University somewhere near me as I fell.'

'Could not the push you felt have been accidental? Crowds can become unruly. Perhaps you were merely the butt of someone's impatience.'

'People don't push others in front of cars just out of impatience,' said the girl tremulously. 'Mother Paul, I want Inspector Savage to know what happened. I—I'm scared!'

'Dear child!' said the Warden, putting out a hand. 'Of course you are frightened. Accidental or intentional, it was a most unnerving experience.'

'And why me?' demanded Elizabeth. 'That is what I can't understand. Peter Baynes was attacked, but that was on account of his film. Why should anyone want to—to harm me?'

The nun did not reply. She lifted the telephone receiver slowly. 'Connect me with Inspector Savage's office,' she said presently. 'Sit down, Elizabeth, and please don't look like that. Nothing is going to happen to you, I promise.' She spoke into the telephone again. 'I wish to speak to Inspector Savage, please. Has he—? Oh, he hasn't returned yet. Will you ask him to get in touch with me as soon as he comes in? The Warden of Brigid Moore Hall. Yes, it's very urgent. Thank you.' Mother Paul replaced the receiver. 'No, he's still in the country. I thought it would take some time,' she added absently.

'In the country!' ejaculated Elizabeth. 'What's he doing in the country at a moment like this?'

'Now, dear, don't worry,' said the Warden soothingly. 'He is still very much concerned with our troubles. But I wouldn't see Professor Craske again—at least, not until we hear what Mr Savage says. Stay where there are plenty of people and I'm sure you need have no fears.'

'There were plenty of people outside that theatre last night,' said Elizabeth bitterly. 'As for Professor Craske—I have no desire to see him again. Now that I've heard from Timothy I can stop pretending I enjoyed his—his practised attentions.' She smiled ruefully at the nun. 'Please don't think I'm unappreciative of your advice concerning Tim and me, but since he has made this overture I am not going to run the risk of further estrangement.'

The Warden beamed in return, but Elizabeth failed to see a sudden excited glint in the usually limpid eyes. 'I'm so happy to hear you say so, dear. Tell me—what overture did Dr Bertram make?'

'I received a note from him,' said Elizabeth, slipping a hand into her pocket. The very touch of the letter gave her a sense of security and happiness. 'He wants me to meet him in the Anthropological museum tonight.'

'The Anthropological museum? That is in the Considine building, is it not?'

Elizabeth nodded. 'The top floor. Wish me luck, Mother Paul. Tim sounds quite abject.'

'Of course I wish you every good fortune, Elizabeth.'

After the girl had gone, Mother Paul sat very still. There was a grave resolute expression on her face. Presently she lifted the telephone receiver again and dialled a number. 'This is the Warden of Brigid Moore Hall speaking. I wish to talk to the Rector, please.'

The warm, humid day had ended with big, steel-coloured clouds banking in the south-eastern sky. As Elizabeth left the Cottage later in the evening, a scatter of raindrops as large as pennies sent her back for a raincoat to cover her pink linen dress. The Considine building was situated at the other side of the University grounds, and she did not want to arrive dripping wet with her hair in unattractive streaks.

It was very dark, the thick clouds of the approaching change blanketing the starlight. A flash of lightning and a low growl of thunder made Elizabeth hasten through the gates. She passed others in the grounds, all making for quick shelter too.

The Considine building loomed up with only a few passage lights burning here and there. She slipped into the foyer, past the caretaker's office and took the automatic lift to the top floor. It was strange that a building, considered inadequate accommodation, could suddenly seem so large and so empty.

The lift came to rest and she waited impatiently for the door to open, hoping to see Timothy standing there with his arms open. If she could just get close to him at once, then there would be no need for words and explanation. But the passage was dim and lonely, and re-echoed to the sound of her footsteps.

'Department of Anthropology museum'—proclaimed a sign above one of the doors. She opened it eagerly. 'Tim! I'm here!'

But the room was in darkness. She felt for the lights, but the switches clicked unresponsively. She held her wrist up to the dim passage light. After ten. Timothy could not have been working in the museum after all, and had only suggested it as a meeting place where they could talk undisturbed. But he was never late as a rule.

She heard the lift doors closing farther down the passage and the hum of its descent, and smiled. Very well! She would be the one waiting with open arms.

A sudden gust of wind seemed to rock the building and handfuls of the penny-sized raindrops rattled against the windows. The change was coming. The atmosphere indoors seemed all the more close and oppressive.

Eagerly, Elizabeth watched the indicator light above the lift door. Now! she thought, smiling in anticipation. Her heart beat fast as the heavy doors slid ponderously aside.

But instead of Timothy, out stepped Margaret Knight.

19

Elizabeth lowered her arms, her smile of welcome fading. But she felt more foolish than disappointed.

Miss Knight gave her a brisk, scornful appraisal. 'Dr Bertram sent me over,' she declared. 'He's been delayed, but you're to wait for him in the museum.'

'The lights won't work,' said Elizabeth, saying the first thing that came into her head in her confusion.

'For land sakes! Not scared of the dark, are you?' said the Manning College housekeeper derisively. 'Let's go and see what the trouble is. I'm used to fixing things. I wasn't raised to be all brain and no brawn.' She led the way down the passage, a small wiry figure topped by a trim cap of white hair.

'H'mm! Looks like a broken fuse,' said Miss Knight, as she snapped the switches unavailingly. 'That's the caretaker's job. Not that I couldn't do it myself, but someone should keep him up to the mark. Talk about a cushy job—why, he wasn't even in his office when I passed! Did you see him, Miss Drew?'

'There was a light on, but I don't remember seeing anyone.'

'That's what I mean!' said the other forthrightly. 'Anyone could sneak in without being seen. I guess no one knows you and me are both up here.'

'I came to see Dr Bertram,' said Elizabeth coldly. 'There was no need for me to account for my movements.'

'My, you do get snooty easily,' remarked Miss Knight, moving across the room. 'Goodness, this place is stuffy—must be all these old Abo things Dr Bertram is so keen on. The caretaker should open a few windows and air the place after hours. That's another job the lazy blighter's missed on.'

She raised a window vigorously and a rush of cool air reached Elizabeth. 'Come on over and see the view, Miss Drew.'

'Yes, it's very fine,' agreed Elizabeth, joining her at the window. 'Did Dr Bertram say how long he would be?'

'I can't say as how he did. But don't worry—I'm here to keep you company.'

'Very kind of you, Margaret,' said the girl dryly. 'But perhaps I won't stay if Dr Bertram is going to be delayed much longer.'

'No, wait!' said the housekeeper quickly. 'Don't you think you owe the poor fellow some of your time? I think it's a downright shame the way you've treated him.'

Elizabeth stiffened. 'Indeed?'

'Downright miserable, he's been. I've been ever so sorry for him.'

'Has Dr Bertram been talking about me—to you?'

'No. As a matter of fact, he hasn't,' the housekeeper admitted, grudgingly. 'I guess he felt there were enough people talking about you already—you and Professor Craske.'

'I find you impertinent, Margaret,' said Elizabeth steadily.

The other shrugged. 'Well, if people behave like you and Dick Craske, they've got to be prepared to take the consequences. Not that I blame him so much. From what I've seen you've thrown yourself at his head. Compromised him, that's what you've done.'

'How dare you speak to me like this!' said Elizabeth angrily.

'Yes, I do dare,' said the other, trenchantly. 'You brainy women think you're so far above me. Well, I've got feelings too—fine feelings when it comes to what a woman should be to a man. And that's all that counts—not a lot of book-learning and degrees and such like. Dick Craske was going along fine. He was free of that stupid sexy wife of his and everything was going to work out well. Then you started chasing him.'

'You've no right to talk like this, Margaret. I know you pride yourself on plain speaking, but you must realize you are being utterly offensive. I won't listen to anything more.'

'Oh, yes, you will!' The housekeeper seized Elizabeth's arm in a small, steely grip. 'You're going to hear me out first. I know what sort of man Dick Craske is—sweet-tongued and full of promises. He'd charm the heart out of any woman. Look at that silly Miss Dove and all those others. He needs protection from himself, Dick does. A good wife who knows how to handle him and make him comfortable—not one of your learned sort with ice-water in their veins and a head stuffed full of stupid learning.'

'I think I see what you mean,' said Elizabeth coldly. 'And now—would you let go of my arm, please?'

But Miss Knight suddenly twisted it round the girl's back. 'You think he doesn't want to marry me?' she demanded harshly. 'Well, you're wrong, see? Heaven knows, he threw out enough hints while Helena was alive. I knew what he meant.'

'Margaret! You're mad—let go of me at once!' The pain up Elizabeth's arm was piercing. Perspiration welled up on her face and was fanned cool by the breeze through the window.

'I wasn't worried about the other women,' said Miss Knight. She was panting, but she held Elizabeth's struggles easily. 'I wasn't even worried about that policeman hanging around. But you—!' She pulled Elizabeth's arm higher and the girl bent forward in agony towards the window sill. 'I'd seen Dick try and make you before. Then when you broke with Dr Bertram, I wondered. But if Dick thinks he can play fast and loose with me now—after all I've done for him!'

Elizabeth's mind clouded with pain. She tried to gather her wits and to call for help, but only a feeble sound escaped her.

'I've got it all worked out—just as I had before. I'm pretty clever, Miss Drew. Much cleverer than all you women with your fancy University educations. That Markham girl—did I run rings round her, the pompous little busy-body! And you fell for the alibi I fixed for myself. Why, I'm much smarter than you. No one will ever guess about Maureen Mornane. That policeman could hang around for years and he still wouldn't know. I've been so clever and I'm not going to wait much longer. If Dick can't wake up to what I've done for him, and what I expect, he'd better look out. He's going to cop the lot if he doesn't play the game by me. I'll work out a way to break his alibi. Didn't I arrange about Helena at a time when I knew he'd be safe just in case something went wrong! I'll think of something. I'm really smart, I am!'

'Timothy! Tim!' moaned Elizabeth, her mind darkening.

'What a fool you are! I typed that letter. I did it in Dr Bertram's own room. I knew you'd fall for it, even though you were playing alley cats with Dick. There's no use you calling out—no one knows we're here. I'm as safe now as I was in that crowd last night, but this time I'm going to make sure.'

Miss Knight jerked savagely at Elizabeth's arm and sent her reeling across the window sill. The lights of the city all around swam under the girl's eyes. She was barely conscious.

From afar off, Miss Knight's ugly voice went on, 'You know what's going to happen when they find you, Miss Drew? There'll be some questions asked—questions like why you committed suicide. On account of her broken engagement they'll say at first. Then it'll come up about how you'd been seeing Dick. Perhaps she killed herself on account of him instead. Then they'll go and ask him all sorts of questions. They'll ask him where he was tonight, and he'll be too scared to reply, because he won't be able to explain why he was near Considine. They wouldn't believe him even if he did say an unknown telephone caller asked him to meet her close by.

'But I'll give him an alibi—that is, if he sees things my way. I'll think of something to clear him. You'll be gone, and he'll be only too glad to turn to me then.'

Elizabeth made a last desperate struggle. Fear was stronger than pain now. She gripped the sill with her free hand.

'Ah, no, you don't!' panted Miss Knight. 'I'm too strong for you. You're going now, Miss Drew. One, two, three, four and then I'll give the final push. You're my fourth—funny how it doesn't worry me! I'd do it again without a qualm. One for Maureen, two for Helena, three for Heather and four—!'

'Miss Knight!'

Suddenly there was a confused pressure of sound in Elizabeth's ears and strong lights stabbed at her clouded eyes. She heard movement and sharp, alarmed voices all about her. Then Margaret's scream of rage as the strain on her arm was ripped away. Long, strong arms were twined about her, wrapping her sagging body close. Somehow she knew they were Timothy's arms. She tried to concentrate on the feel of them and of Timothy's heart thudding under her cheek. In that way she was able to smother out Margaret Knight's last horrible cry as the woman flung herself head first from the window . . .

20

'I knew Dr Bertram could not have written that letter to you, Elizabeth,' explained the Warden. 'He had promised me most faithfully not to get in touch with you. Such an honourable-looking man—I knew I could trust him.'

Elizabeth turned shadowed eyes on her reinstated fiancé, who had wriggled uncomfortably at Mother Paul's guileless compliments. 'You knew all along that I was only seeing Richard Craske at Mother Paul's suggestion, Timothy, how could you be so—so dishonourable!'

He laughed and raised the hand he had been holding unashamedly to his lips. The nun regarded them dotingly. 'I didn't know when you flung your ring in my face,' he protested. 'I thought you really meant it. You've no idea what I went through that night. Don't do anything like that to me again, will you!'

'Of course she won't,' said Mother Paul comfortingly. 'For one thing there won't be the opportunity now that you are going to be married very soon. The Centre will be just the place for Elizabeth to get over her horrid experiences. So nice and flat and no cars to run her down. You'll have a delightful honeymoon.'

'Yes, I think we might,' agreed Timothy, as though the idea was a new one. 'What about it, darling? A wedding in Manning College chapel and then the expedition.'

'I'd love it,' returned Elizabeth, flashing a warm grateful smile at the Warden.

'Then that is settled,' said Mother Paul, beaming at them fondly. 'Such a relief, for it doesn't do to scheme with the lives of others as I have been these last days. Elizabeth, you guessed that I sent Dr Bertram to Professor Craske's house on purpose, but I had another motive other than to—to make him annoyed. I wanted Margaret Knight to know where you were.'

'So that is what you meant by killing two birds with one stone! And what you meant, Timothy, when you said a message was conveyed to you about where I was, Mother Paul deliberately told Margaret to tell you.'

The Warden continued in an apologetic voice, 'So shocking of me to say so, but the breaking of your engagement was a piece of good fortune I had dared to hope for. Miss Knight's jealousy was seriously aroused.'

'And so you encouraged me to keep seeing Richard not so much to make Timothy jealous as Margaret?'

'Yes, dear, I'm afraid so. Such a horrid scheme, but I could think of no other way. Naturally after your sad quarrel Dr Bertram tried to see you the very next day. So fortunate that I was able to intercept him. We had quite an interesting little chat, did we not. Doctor?'

'Very interesting,' he agreed dryly. 'You told me, in effect, that you were using Elizabeth as a kind of bait, and that unless I did as you told me your plans to trap a murderer would be ruined.'

'Yes, you took a great deal of persuading,' admitted Mother Paul, a twinkle in her eye.

'I would call it coercion,' retorted Timothy, grinning at her. 'However, I promised not to get in touch with Elizabeth until you gave the word. That word came late yesterday afternoon through the Rector.'

'Yes, I had to ask him to play liaison. I was so anxious about not arousing Margaret's suspicions. If she heard my asking to speak to you on the telephone, she might have guessed that Elizabeth had told me of your alleged note. I felt so sure after her first attempt on Elizabeth's life that this time she was really intending to be successful. I think she more or less acted on the spur of the moment that night she followed Elizabeth and Professor Craske to the city; in a fit of insane jealousy because of seeing them together. That push she gave in the crowd was a hit and miss attempt. But this plan to lure Elizabeth to the top floor of the Considine building was more deadly.

'I had to count on Inspector Savage being back in time, and he was, bless him! Such a trial I have been to that good man. I gave him no time to report on the trip I had made him take to the country. He merely gave me one of his long-suffering looks and took his men over to Considine without question.'

'We were there for two hours before you arrived, Elizabeth,' said Timothy ruefully. 'I had a position squatting behind a bunch of firesticks.'

'Then it was Mr Savage who broke the fuse of the museum lights?'

'Well, there were about six husky males to stay hidden until the crucial moment. Savage said no one was to move until he spoke.' Timothy suddenly gripped Elizabeth's hand tightly.

'It was the hardest thing I've ever had to do—stay quiet while that awful woman—!' he broke off, pressing her hand against his face. Elizabeth put up her hand and touched his hair fleetingly.

'Well, never mind! It's all over now,' said Mother Paul cheerfully. 'And now, I do believe that is Inspector Savage at last.'

She had seen him approaching through the parlour windows and went out swiftly to let him into the house.

Savage held out his hand, a smile twisting his mouth. 'Well, Mother Paul?' He had a speech of congratulation and appreciation all ready and was rather taken aback when the nun said hurriedly, 'Do you mind if we take a little while to return to the parlour? Dear Elizabeth and that excessively nice man she is going to marry! Such stringent chaperonage in an establishment like this.'

His eyes twinkled. 'I can see you are more interested in match-making than in murder at the moment.'

'I am so grateful to you for allowing Dr Bertram to rescue Elizabeth,' said the Warden earnestly. 'He will never forget the mortal danger she was in, while she will always remember that he saved her life.'

'I cannot imagine a firmer basis for married happiness,' he replied, solemnly.

Mother Paul coughed delicately before opening the parlour door. Elizabeth and Timothy were sitting farther apart on the couch, but the girl's face was a delightful glowing pink and Timothy was carefully replacing his breast-pocket handkerchief.

Savage regarded them quizzically. 'Feeling better after your ordeal, Miss Drew? You've been a brave girl.'

He turned to the Warden. 'I have just come from Professor Craske. He insists he knew nothing.'

'Do you believe that?'

The inspector shrugged. 'I'd say the same if I were in his shoes.

There is no doubt in my mind that he was suspicious of his wife's death, but to admit it would make him an accessory after the fact. Especially as he was, in truth, glad to be free of her.'

'Yes, he knew,' said Elizabeth quietly. 'I told him the other night why you were here, Inspector. He was frightened, but not surprised. Do you think he realized it was Margaret?'

'No, I doubt that. Probably Miss Dove was the one he had in mind. Evidently he finds it difficult to recall all the women to whom he has given reason for hope,' added Savage dryly.

'Do sit down, Inspector,' invited the Warden. 'I want to hear about your investigations at Ararat. I was so thankful it wasn't a wild goose chase or should I have said a mare's nest? Ah, poor Miss Dove!'

'I must admit I was sceptical right up to the end,' confessed Savage. 'Even with the actual order of exhumation in my hand, I was still doubtful whether to go through with it.'

'Yes, I know,' said Mother Paul sympathetically. 'Such an odd notion of mine. But I felt sure that it was the only place where poor little Maureen Mornane could be. So kind of you to believe me, Inspector.'

'Kind!' ejaculated Savage, giving the others an expressive glance. He laughed shortly. 'Mother Paul, you don't seem to realize that but for you this case would never have been solved.'

'I was in a fortunate position,' said the nun swiftly. 'So easy to see things in an unbiased light when one is new to an environment. You must remember that everyone else had actually seen a student who went by the name of Maureen Mornane.'

Elizabeth leaned forward. 'Are you saying that there was no such person as Maureen?' she asked, bewildered.

'Oh, by no means, dear! But the Maureen you knew here at Brigid Moore was actually Margaret Knight!

'Margaret! You mean she murdered Maureen and then impersonated her?'

The Warden nodded. 'That naughty rag by the Manning undergraduates gave me the notion that maybe Maureen Mornane wasn't actually Maureen at all. The Baynes boy with the red wig and the freckle spots—quite ridiculous, of course, but he did manage to convey the idea of Maureen. I could not help thinking of the possibility of a more serious impersonation. The limp, the freckles, the red hair, a certain familiarity with University life—and who was there to know it wasn't Maureen Mornane, the Florence Ryall scholar from Mulgoa via Ararat?

'Then I remembered what Judith had told me of her sister and what her tutors had thought of the supposed Maureen—well, it just seemed like two different persons. Which, of course, was the case. So you see, Inspector, when Miss Drew and I came to consult you on the disappearance I was already on the way to the truth. The letter from Maureen and the telegram which Margaret must have sent in her name to make it appear she had arrived at Brigid Moore seemed to endorse my rather extravagant theory.'

'Why didn't you tell me of your theory then?' asked Savage.

The nun replied shrewdly. 'Would you have believed me? That poor man in the Missing Persons Bureau was all for giving me short shrift, and I couldn't blame him. So patient and polite of you to listen with such close attention, Inspector.' She beamed on him warmly. 'I told you then I was most grateful and I still am.'

Savage felt himself reddening for the first time in his long, tough career. 'Perhaps if anyone else had come with the same story, I might not have been so patient,' he admitted, laughing.

'Quite so. Poor little Judith. I daresay if I had been Warden for a long time, I too would have dismissed her wild accusations.'

A knock at the parlour door made Mother Paul turn her head. 'That will be Judith now. I sent for her so that you could tell her about her sister. Come in, child!'

Savage got up and went forward. 'Hullo, Judith!' he said gently, taking her hand. He led her to a chair, where she sat with wide, sad eyes.

'Inspector Savage wants to tell you about Maureen, dear,' said Mother Paul. 'Miss Drew and Dr Bertram only know part of the story, but as they have been so closely involved, I feel they are entitled to hear it too. After that, I'm sure Inspector Savage will want us to refrain from discussing the matter further.'

Savage nodded briefly. 'I've been in consultation with the Vice-Chancellor, and he agreed with the desirability of hushing the case up as much as possible.'

Judith looked at him. 'Maureen is dead, isn't she? She's been dead for a long time.'

'Yes, she's been dead for over a year, Judith. You were right all the time. She was murdered.'

'By that Miss Knight, of Manning College?' asked the girl timidly. 'Everyone has been talking about—about the accident. She didn't really fall out of a window, did she?'

'Never mind about that, Judith.'

'I won't say anything—I promise. But why—why did she kill Maureen? She couldn't have known her.'

'She knew Maureen—briefly. She met your sister on the train travelling to Ararat.'

'On the train? But Maureen was here at Brigid Moore! Everyone knew her before she disappeared—Fiona, Monica—'

'Maureen never arrived at the University, Judith. It was Miss Knight pretending to be Maureen. Listen to me closely and I'll try to tell you what happened. You have often heard people say how they wished they could be in two places at once?'

The girl nodded uncertainly.

'Well, that is what Margaret Knight did by assuming your sister's identity. Towards the end of the summer vacation over a year ago, Miss Knight was summoned to the death-bed of an only relative in the small country town of Audleigh. You know where that is, Judith?'

'Yes—on the line between our town, Mulgoa and Ararat.'

'Miss Knight's relative had died and she was on her way to Ararat to make funeral arrangements. By chance she got into the same compartment as a young red-haired girl who was in the process of writing a letter in order to while away the tedium of the journey. You said your sister was a bright, friendly girl, Judith. Soon she and Miss Knight got talking, and when Maureen learned her travelling companion actually lived at one of the University colleges, she quickly put away her letter. Mother Paul observed the clue of this letter.'

The nun nodded. 'The abruptness with which Maureen finished her letter seemed to indicate that she had found something better to entertain her. Then there were her words—*I'll write later. I'll know more about the University then*. Taking these facts together, it could only mean that someone had entered her compartment who knew about University life. When Miss Knight was questioned as to the genuineness of her call to the country, she told Inspector Savage the name of the town where her relative died.' Mother Paul paused and dived a hand into her skirt pocket. 'I made a point of writing down whatever information Elizabeth passed on to me,' she said, rifling through the pages of her little red book. 'Yes, here it is—Audleigh! I looked it up on the map and found, as Judith has just told us, that it is on the branch line to Ararat.

'The telegram which Maureen was supposed to have sent on arrival here was typical of any telegram. Anyone could have sent it.'

Elizabeth leaned forward. 'Then you must have known it was Margaret quite early.'

The Warden looked over her glasses. 'She gave herself away the first and only time I met the unfortunate creature,' she announced simply.

'You mean the night we went to Manning to check on that telephone call from Heather?'

'Yes, don't you recall, dear? Judith was with us. Don't you remember Miss Knight's saying that Judith looked just like her sister? Now how could she possibly have been in a position to make that comparison? During the short time Maureen was at Brigid Moore, Miss Knight was attending a relative's obsequies over two hundred miles away, or so everyone had been led to believe. If she knew Judith resembled her sister, then when and where did she know Maureen?

'Of course, I couldn't quite understand why Miss Knight should want to commit murder, at first. It was only after a most informative discussion with Elizabeth that I was able to gain some insight into Professor Craske's character.'

'Professor Craske?' interrupted Judith timidly. 'I don't understand. What had Miss Knight's impersonation of Maureen to do with Professor Craske?'

Savage glanced at the nun uncertainly. 'Shall I continue, Mother Paul?'

'Please do! An unpleasant, sordid business, but Judith is a sensible child—are you not, my dear?'

Savage turned to the student. 'That chance meeting on the train with your sister gave Miss Knight an idea—a wicked, terrible idea, which presently she put into execution. Miss Knight was infatuated with Professor Craske who was married to a woman allegedly an invalid. She was frequently at his house as a nurse-companion to Mrs Craske, and in some way or other became convinced that Professor Craske would be willing to return her passion but for his married state.'

Judith's eyes grew wider. 'You mean Miss Knight killed Mrs Craske too?'

Savage nodded. 'Getting rid of Mrs Craske was her primary purpose. But she wanted to do it in such a way as to render both herself and Professor Craske above suspicion, should her plan of accidental drowning be doubted. She knew Mrs Craske's habits well—the heavy sedatives she took, the time of bath, etc. A telephone call about a non-existent parcel at the registrar's office kept the maid, Thelma, out of the way. After drowning Mrs Craske, she went straight to Spencer Street railway station and collected the luggage she had booked through from Ararat. Then in the ladies' cloakroom, or some other convenient place, she threw off the impersonation of Maureen Mornane and became Miss Knight, the housekeeper of Manning College, just back from burying her aunt in the country.'

'Then Maureen was used just as a—means,' said Judith tremulously. 'It could have been anyone.'

'Not quite. Here was a girl with certain easy-to-imitate features on her way to a University college situated right next door to the proposed victim. If Miss Knight could only take her place for a day or two the murder of Mrs Craske could be accomplished in perfect safety. Even if she was seen going into the Craske house—which, in fact, happened—no one would think to associate the housekeeper of Manning College with the red-haired freshette from Brigid Moore who subsequently disappeared without trace.'

Judith suddenly covered her face with her hands. 'Horrible! Horrible!'

'Hush, child! Would you rather Inspector Savage did not continue?'

Judith uncovered her tear-stained face. 'No, please go on! I'm sorry to be so—so weak. Did you—did you find Maureen—her body, I mean?'

Savage said gently, 'Yes, I found Maureen's body. Mother Paul guessed where it would be.'

'Where did you find her?'

'In a grave, Judith, in the cemetery of a small town called Audleigh.'

'Audleigh? The place where Miss Knight's relative—? You mean she—?'

Elizabeth found herself gripping Timothy's hand tightly. 'Judith, you don't really want to know,' she said unsteadily.

'Yes, I do,' cried the girl passionately. 'Tell me, Inspector.'

Savage exchanged another glance with the Warden. 'Very well,' he agreed quietly. 'This is what I think happened, and it is borne out by the inquiries I made the last two days. Having made up her mind to use Maureen, Miss Knight persuaded her to book in at an hotel in Ararat, suggesting that they travel down to Melbourne together the following day. While Maureen was doing this, Miss Knight went to call on an undertaker to arrange her aunt's funeral. I interviewed this undertaker and obtained two valuable pieces of information from him. The first was that while only one woman came to him to make funeral arrangements, she was later accompanied by a young girl when he picked her up by arrangement to go out to Audleigh. The second was the size of the coffin. Miss Knight told the undertaker that she was in a hurry to finalize matters. In order to save time by avoiding to and fro trips from Ararat to Audleigh she gave him the necessary information regarding her aunt's corpse—which was probably her original and quite genuine idea. However, when the undertaker actually came to see the body, it did not seem to warrant the large-sized coffin upon which Miss Knight had insisted. He could not give me the precise movements of the two women when they reached the deceased's house in Audleigh, but he admitted losing sight of the younger one before the actual interment.'

Savage knew that Judith had realized the truth, so he did not go into the details of the exhumation and the discovery of the second body in the coffin—strangled and stripped of all clothing.

After a pause, he continued. 'Back in Ararat, Miss Knight went to the railway station, booked her own baggage through to Melbourne, changed into Maureen's clothes and then proceeded unobtrusively to the hotel. Here she dyed her hair red and experimented with make-up so as to appear freckled. You might recall that Miss Knight had a small figure and her face was round and quite young-looking when you disregarded her hair. On the following morning the hotel people saw a red-haired girl with a slight limp leave with her case for the station.

'Miss Knight's biggest test was when she arrived at Brigid Moore, but she knew enough about the University to count on a certain amount of confusion at the beginning of term and the fact that freshettes are normally shy and unsure. She resolved to remain as unobtrusive as possible.

'But one student tried to break through her reticence—Heather Markham. We know that Heather went to see the alleged Maureen in her room while she was unpacking. She failed to make headway with Miss Knight, but she observed some clue which later on came back to her.'

'An article of clothing,' declared Mother Paul. 'I should say one of those scarves girls tie over their heads. Miss Knight must have been careful to keep her distinctive hair covered in between the time she left Ararat station after donning the real Maureen's clothes and the hotel room where she dyed her hair. The mistake she made was to use a scarf of her own.

'When the Manning undergraduates planned their rag they naturally turned for props to the housekeeper of their college. That fatal head scarf on Peter Baynes attracted Heather's attention. Where had she seen it before? Gradually she remembered. But what was it doing on a Manning undergraduate, when she had seen it last in Maureen Mornane's possession? Realizing that the boys probably borrowed their clothes from Miss Knight, she decided to get in touch with the housekeeper. Although she was far from guessing the danger of her curiosity, she secretly rang Manning College from the call-box in Cemetery Road.'

'Then Heather must have spoken to Margaret at two after all,' put in Elizabeth.

'That is so. And Miss Knight made up the story of the later telephone call so as to give herself an alibi—just as she let it be known that Heather rang merely to complain about the rag.'

'She made a point of telling me at the Manning reception. I realize that now. And there is something else I remember—the cakes!'

'What about the cakes?' asked Mother Paul, with interest. 'I recall

Miss Knight's telling us that she had been out to get them for the reception before Heather rang.'

'But that was not what Margaret told me originally,' said Elizabeth. 'She complained about Heather's phone call delaying her from getting out to buy the cakes. How stupid of me not to notice the inconsistency until now!'

Judith said shyly, 'I should have guessed something of the truth when Heather said that the rag wasn't such a bad thing after all. And not being able to find the—the mark of the Mornanes.'

Elizabeth smiled at her. 'Neither of us would make a detective, Judith.'

'It's a matter of observing the little odd things that happen,' explained Mother Paul earnestly. 'As soon as Miss Knight heard what Heather had to say, she knew she was in some danger. She made up her mind at once to get rid of her. After all, she had already committed two murders without arousing suspicion—or so she fondly imagined. She had become conceited enough to disregard the odd rumours from Brigid Moore Hall and Inspector Savage's presence at the University. But she made slips—small ones admittedly, but to anyone on the lookout, these slips meant something.'

Mother Paul paused to consult her notebook again. 'For example, when she came face to face with Professor Whipple leaving the Craske house. According to the Dean, the red-haired student turned and ran! Miss Knight must have been concerned about possible recognition and forgot Maureen's limp . . . Then there was the matter of Professor Craske's raincoat.'

'You mean it was Margaret who returned it?'

'She saw it in the cupboard where she had put poor little Heather. On no account did she want any sort of suspicion to fall on Professor Craske, so she took it back to his house at once. It was then that she saw the neglected state of his living-room, and very foolishly sent one of her maids over the next day.'

Elizabeth looked at the nun with affectionate admiration. 'Yes, I told you about Thelma's saying Miss Knight had sent her, but I did not realize the significance. So it was Margaret whom Peter Baynes heard climbing the fence!'

'She probably knew about his working in our garden and she had arranged to meet Heather in the Cottage. Poor Heather was quite un-suspicious about this meeting. She was puzzled about the scarf, but that was all. However, if Miss Knight wanted to speak with her spe-cially, Heather was only too glad to be her confidante. The poor child liked to be looked upon as a helping hand. Miss Knight had only to pretend to be in trouble concerning Maureen's disappearance and to appeal for advice, and she had Heather exactly where she wanted her.

'Under the pretext of Heather being more capable of writing out a statement of what she knew about Maureen, Miss Knight obtained a passable suicide note. With the girl's back turned, Miss Knight slipped off her belt and strangled her. But here again she made slips—and far graver ones. Heather's wide belt and the high position in which she was found hanging in the cupboard made a verdict of suicide impos-sible to accept.'

'This time there was no doubt about a murder having been com-mitted,' put in Savage grimly. 'I no longer had any misgivings about accepting Mother Paul's story that two earlier murders had been com-mitted. Unfortunately,' a dry note crept into his voice. 'I had over-done the scepticism. I think Mother Paul wanted to punish me a little, and so she withheld the theory she had already evolved in her own mind concerning Maureen Mornane.'

The Warden looked distressed. 'Believe me, Inspector,' she said earnestly, 'that was not my intention at all. I just had to wait for something to substantiate my theory. I couldn't ask you to go dig-ging up strange coffins on the off-chance, so to speak. But when Peter Baynes's film was stolen, which, incidentally had to be accomplished well away from Manning to avoid suspicion, it became obvious that Judith was being prevented from catching this glimpse of her alleged sister. The only possible reason for this was that the Maureen in the film was not Maureen at all.' The Warden gazed at Savage and made a gesture of appeal. 'You do understand, don't you?'

The inspector's eyes twinkled. He got up and took Mother Paul's extended hand in his big one. 'If I felt chastised, then it was no more than I deserved, Mother Paul.'

She rose too, in a rustle of serge skirts and rosary beads. 'What you deserve is the undying thanks of everyone at the University,' she said warmly, returning the pressure of his handshake.

'Don't forget it was my suggestion that you should go to the police,' murmured Timothy, as though putting in a claim for recognition.

'Then the Whipples had nothing to do with the case,' said Elizabeth thoughtfully. 'But you were interested in Mrs Whipple, Mother Paul, especially in the—er—colour of her hair.'

'Just a little hint, dear,' explained the Warden apologetically. 'I couldn't resist it. Didn't it start you thinking?'

'You had already given me enough to think about,' replied Elizabeth ruefully. 'And the time you almost had Fiona saying Judith was Maureen? Was that another hint?'

'Not altogether. Fiona brought out an important clue. Her memory of Maureen was that she was taller than Judith, whereas Judith had told me that she was shorter.'

Inspector Savage prepared to leave. He shook hands with Elizabeth and Timothy and wished them luck. Then he turned to Judith who was standing close to the Warden. She looked back at him steadfastly.

Just a slip of a girl, he thought. It had taken pluck—pluck and Mother Paul. 'Good-bye, Judith,' he said gently. 'Maureen knows what you have done for her. It is for you now to leave the mark of the Mornanes on Brigid Moore Hall—a special mark for which she will be watching!'

THE END

MORE BOOKS BY JUNE WRIGHT

RESERVATION FOR MURDER

June Wright had already published several highly praised mysteries before she created her most memorable detective, the Reverend Mother Mary St Paul of the Cross. Mother Paul may seem distracted or absentminded, but nothing important escapes her attention—she turns out to have a shrewd grasp of everything that's going on beneath the surface of events.

In *Reservation for Murder*, the first of three mysteries featuring this unlikely and endearing heroine, the kindly nun is in charge of a residential hostel for young women working in offices and shops in Melbourne. Many of the women have received nasty anonymous letters, and an atmosphere of suspicion and accusation has spread throughout the house. When Mary Allen finds a stranger stabbed to death in the garden, and a few days later one of the residents is found drowned, an apparent suicide, the tension reaches fever pitch. Is there a connection between the two deaths? Or between them and the poison-pen letters? The police investigation, abetted by the resourceful Mary Allen, proceeds in fits and starts, but meanwhile Mother Paul pursues her own enquiries.

DUCK SEASON DEATH

June Wright wrote this lost gem in the mid-1950s, but consigned it to her bottom drawer after her publisher foolishly rejected it. Perhaps it was just a little ahead of its time, because while it delivers a bravura twist on the classic 'country house' murder mystery, it's also a sharp-eyed and sparkling send-up of the genre.

When someone takes advantage of a duck hunt to murder publisher Athol Sefton at a remote hunting inn, it soon turns out that almost everyone, guests and staff alike, had good reason to shoot him. Sefton's nephew Charles believes he can solve the crime by applying the traditional "rules of the game" he's absorbed over years as a reviewer of detective fiction. Much to his annoyance, however, the killer doesn't seem to be playing by those rules, and Charles finds that he is the one under suspicion. *Duck Season Death* is a both a devilishly clever whodunit and a delightful entertainment.

MURDER IN THE TELEPHONE EXCHANGE

When an unpopular colleague at Melbourne Central is murdered, Maggie Byrnes resolves to turn sleuth. Some of her co-workers are acting strangely, and Maggie is convinced she has a better chance of figuring out the killer's identity than the stodgy police team assigned to the case, who seem to think she herself might have had something to do with it. But then one of her friends is murdered too, and it looks like Maggie is next in line.

This is a mystery in the tradition of Dorothy L. Sayers, full of verve and wit. It also offers an evocative account of Melbourne in the early postwar years, as young women flocked to the big city, leaving behind small-town life for jobs, boarding houses and independence.

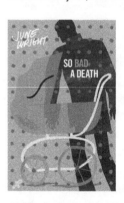

SO BAD A DEATH

When *Murder in the Telephone Exchange* was reissued in 2014, June Wright was hailed by the *Sydney Morning Herald* as "our very own Agatha Christie," and a new generation of readers fell in love with her blend of intrigue and psychological suspense – and with her winning sleuth, Maggie Byrnes. Maggie returns to the fray in *So Bad a Death*. She's married now, living in a Melbourne suburb, yet violent death dogs her footsteps even in apparently tranquil Middleburn. It's no surprise when a widely disliked local bigwig (who happens to be her landlord) is shot, but Maggie suspects someone is also targeting the infant who is his heir. Her compulsion to investigate puts everyone she loves in danger. Includes Lucy Sussex's fascinating 1996 interview with June Wright.

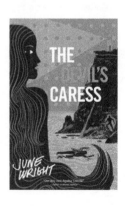

THE DEVIL'S CARESS

A classic country-house mystery with an emotional intensity worthy of Daphne du Maurier. Overworked young medic Marsh Mowbray has been invited to the weekend home of her revered mentor, Dr. Kate Waring, on the wild southern coast of the Mornington Peninsula outside Melbourne. Marsh is hoping to get some much-needed rest, but her stay turns out to be anything but relaxing. As storms rage outside, the house on the cliff's edge seethes with hatred and tension. Two suspicious deaths follow in quick succession, and there is no shortage of suspects. "Doubt is the devil's caress,", one of the characters tells Marsh, as her resolute efforts to get to the bottom of the deaths force her to question everyone's motives, including those of Dr. Kate.